WHERE THE BLUEBELLS GROW WILD

Stephen employs Sara, a landscape designer, to improve the appearance of the gardens of Knowles House, his Georgian mansion. He wants to use innovative ideas to generate additional sources of income and is hoping to hire it out for special events — an attractive garden would boost his chances. Lucy, Stephen's childhood friend, lives with her father on the adjoining country estate. Everyone thinks Lucy and Stephen are made for each other — but then along comes Sara . . .

Books by Wendy Kremer
in the Linford Romance Library:

REAP THE WHIRLWIND

WENDY KREMER

WHERE THE BLUEBELLS GROW WILD

Complete and Unabridged

LINFORD
Leicester

First published in Great Britain in 2008

First Linford Edition
published 2010

British Library CIP Data

Kremer, Wendy.
    Where the bluebells grow wild. - -
(Linford romance library)
    1. Women gardeners- -Fiction. 2. Landscape
gardening- -Fiction. 3. Love stories.
    4. Large type books.
    I. Title II. Series
    823.9′2–dc22

ISBN 978–1–44480–224–5

Published by
F. A. Thorpe (Publishing)
Anstey, Leicestershire

Set by Words & Graphics Ltd.
Anstey, Leicestershire
Printed and bound in Great Britain by
T. J. International Ltd., Padstow, Cornwall

This book is printed on acid-free paper

1

As Sara Maxwell was climbing the steps to the flat-roofed portico, a tall man came round the corner. He hesitated for a moment when he saw her before he increased his pace. Sara had a couple of seconds to study him before he reached her.

His voice was deep and pleasant, and he gave her the beginnings of an apologetic smile when he said. 'I'm afraid the house and gardens are not open to the public at present.'

Her eyes twinkled and she eyed him confidently. 'I know. I have an appointment, with Mr Stephen Dumont.'

His dark eyebrows lifted and then he held out his hand. 'You've found him. You must be Miss/Mrs Maxwell? Forgive me — I was under the misguided assumption that S. Maxwell would be a man!' He had an aesthetic appearance, with an aristocratic thin nose, well-formed lips, large dark eyes, and thick dark-brown hair tapering neatly to his collar.

Sara took his hand; it was warm and firm. 'Good morning, Mr Dumont! People often assume that garden-designers are men. Probably because they think the job is synonymous with lots of physical work! I'm Sara Maxwell — Miss!'

He nodded briskly but his expression was not unfriendly. 'Let's go inside to my study.' He strode ahead and opened one section of the double-winged entrance door. He stood aside to let her pass.

Sara walked onwards, and was impressed by the beautiful proportions of the large entrance hall. Facing her was a grand staircase; its sides bordered with intricate wrought-iron work. A flight of wide marble steps rose to a mid-level landing and then continued on to the left and the right, up to the second floor. The elegance of the Georgian Period was evident in the whole room — the elaborate plaster-work, the long eight-paned windows, and the niches around the hallway housing classical statues. 'What a beautiful room!'

He was right behind her; 'Yes, isn't it?' His firm mouth curled as if it was on the edge of a smile. 'My office is through here.' He preceded her, opening one of the doors that led off the hall.

Sara found herself in a large book-lined room. Comfortable armchairs were positioned each side of the ornate fireplace, and logs were piled in the fire-basket ready for lighting. Heavy brocade curtains framed the paned-windows, and the huge desk in the centre dominated the remaining space.

Stephen Dumont motioned her towards a chair. 'Please take a seat.' He moved behind the desk, sat down and began to shuffle papers together. He waited until she'd settled then he came straight to the point. 'From our correspondence you'll know why you're here. In a nut-shell, I want to improve the gardens. They've lacked any real attention for some time, as you may have noticed.'

Sara's nervousness subsided as she came to terms with the situation and her surroundings. She nodded under-standingly, without commenting.

He continued. 'We have one chap who cuts the lawns and tries to keep the tree and shrub growth under control, but he only comes two days a week so he's fully occupied already.' Stephen leaned back into the high leather chair; it creaked softly. 'You'll appreciate that running a house like this gets more expensive with every passing year, and labour costs are not likely to come down in the future. The repair work and inheritance tax will be a nightmare for whoever follows me.'

He picked up a thick-barrelled foun-tain pen with gold trimmings, and his slender fingers played with it as he spoke. He had a powerful set of shoulders and looked tough, lean and sinewy.

It seemed bizarre to Sara that he was so concerned about things that might not happen or with thoughts about death when he was still young and full of life, but then, she didn't have his responsibilities. She had to concentrate her attention, drag her eyes away from his hands, and focus on his face.

'I've decided we must generate more income; open the house for special events like conferences, weddings, family celebrations, that sort of thing. This is where your company comes in; upgrading the gardens will enhance the appearance of the place and hopefully awaken people's interest all the more. Any improvements have to be achieved on a shoestring budget, and cause as little upheaval as possible. The gardens also need to be low-maintenance afterwards, so that I don't need to pour any profit I make, back into the upkeep.'

She met his glance steadily. The dark blue trouser suit and crisp white blouse heightened the translucence of her face and neck; she was not conscious of it, but he thought she made a very attractive picture as she listened attentively.

Sara decided it was appropriate to comment. 'Unfortunately a lot of large private houses seem to be ending up as hotels, golf-clubs or schools these days because they have become an impossible financial burden.'

His lips stiffened faintly. 'I hope that won't happen to Knowles House; certainly not in my lifetime. I want to control who uses it and what for, as long as I possibly can.'

Sara smiled reassuringly. 'I can understand why. Now I know what you want, I'd like to walk around the gardens to get some ideas. When I've worked things out, including the costs, we can perhaps meet again?'

Stephen Dumont studied her attractive face. It was framed by curly light-auburn hair. Her eyes were hazel, more green than brown, her make up was subtle, and her skin was creamy and free of blemishes. He liked what he saw, and she had the right attitude; she was professional but not pushy. He nodded. 'That sounds like a sensible idea. Phone me when you're ready, and we'll fix another appointment.'

Sara relaxed and felt at ease with him. He was an attractive cultivated man, owner of an estate and large Georgian mansion, but there was nothing arrogant or haughty in his manner. 'I'll try not to disturb your present layout too much when I make my suggestions, and I'll only make additions or changes when I think they'll be beneficial and will justify the financial outlay.'

He put the fountain pen down, and was reassured. She understood what he wanted. 'Good, that's it exactly!'

'Will you fill in a few essential points for me? I noticed the garden is walled. How big is it exactly?'

'The garden? Roughly six acres.'

'Do you know who planned it?' Sara mused he was very attractive to look at;

women would definitely find him very alluring.

He tilted his head and a slow smile covered his face. 'I suppose someone did plan it; planted the oaks, the beeches and all the rest. Someone must have levelled off some areas and raised other sections, even I can tell it isn't all just a whim of nature, but I suspect that the garden evolved from the amount of interest any particular generation decided to give it. My mother might be able to tell you more; I can't help much I'm afraid.'

'It doesn't matter. The house is Georgian, and you want to accentuate its beauty.' He opened his mouth to speak, but she felt so relaxed in his company now that she added quickly. 'It has to be easy-care and done as cheaply as possible!'

Something twinkled in his eyes. 'Exactly! Do you want me to show you around?'

'I'd rather wander on my own, if you have no objections?' She studied his face and decided he was more than just attractive; he had a charisma that probably resulted from a combination of his background, his upbringing, and his character. Sara wondered why she was so interested. She was here to get a commission to redesign the garden; the man Stephen Dumont was of secondary interest. She concentrated on his reply.

'Not at all. In fact it suits me fine, as I must return to the estate office as soon as possible — another visitor. Take your time! If you have any other queries or need more information, I'm in the old stable buildings, at the back of the house.'

Sara got up, and he followed. 'I'll be in touch soon, Mr Dumont.' Shouldering her bag, she followed him and they retraced their way through the hall.

* * *

The day was invigorating and mild breezes swept through her hair as she began to examine the gardens and surroundings. The house itself was at least half a mile from the public road running through the valley.

Other trees were dotted throughout the garden; mostly oaks, limes and beeches but there were a couple of exotic ones — clearly someone in the family had travelled, and brought their interest in unusual plants back to this corner of England. In the middle distance, beyond the public road and concealed by trees and the fold of the valley, was the small village where she'd booked a room for the night in the local pub.

The position of the house was well chosen. She looked at it; typically Georgian, it displayed excellent proportions and symmetry. The eight-paned windows on all sides had limestone lintels, and there were gabled dormers high up in the roof. Its simplicity and elegance were pleasing to look at.

Sara walked along a gravelled pathway that circumnavigated the house, to see the views from all sides. On the way she noticed a tennis court, surrounded by an ugly net fence. She found there were grassy lawns bordering the mansion everywhere and there were already several excellent views that only needed some more emphasis.

There were some former cob-barns nearby. They'd been turned into living quarters, probably for estate workers. She only found one flowerbed; it was below a stone balustrade running the length of one side of the house. It was filled with perennial flowers that were interspersed with evergreen shrubs. Half way along it, some shallow steps led up to the stone terrace directly in front of the main building.

As she walked, she took lots of digital photos. Some time later, sitting in her car she made some quick guesses. Accurate measurements would only be necessary if they got the job. She typed her impressions and immediate ideas into her notebook.

Her boss, Brian, had been running

Designs and Possibilities for nearly ten years; it had a very good reputation. Sara had been with him for two years and Brian promised she could handle this job on her own — if she got it. He was very busy with other assignments.

Sara knew she'd need to impress Stephen Dumont with her ideas and convince him that she was capable of turning them into reality. He was the type of owner who'd examine every suggestion carefully before he made a final decision.

A couple of weeks later Sara sat facing Stephen once more. Her plans, proposals, and cost estimations were spread out on the desk. He was studying them carefully.

'Umm! It's hard for me to imagine what trees, etc. will look like from these plans. I'm not much of a botanist.'

She took a glossy publication out of her briefcase. 'I've brought you a catalogue showing the trees and plants I'd like to use.' She handed it to him across the desk with an extra sheet of paper. 'I've given any new trees or plants in the plans a number, and made a list of the names to correspond with those numbers. The names are in the catalogue's alphabetic appendix, where you'll find a picture.'

Stephen took the glossy booklet from her and placed the single typed sheet to the side. He flipped through the pages and referred back to her list while studying the suggestions and drawings. Sara grew more nervous as time went on, even though she knew she'd done a good job. The only sound in the room, apart from the rustle of paper across the desk, was the ticking of the clock in the corner.

Finally he looked up and leaned forward slightly. 'I'd like to keep these for a couple of days. I'd like to check things on the exact spot.'

Sara was pleased; at least he hadn't rejected things outright. She nodded. 'Of course.'

He pointed to one item. 'I notice you've marked the tennis court in red, why? I hope you haven't suggested I should get rid of it?'

She shook her head softly in answer. 'But the framework and netting is ugly. Its appearance can't be ignored; it's too near the house. I thought you could improve things by knocking a couple of feet off the framework and using modern netting, which is extremely strong and almost invisible from a distance. If a couple of mature trees were planted around at irregular intervals and some shrubs positioned in-between, the overall picture would improve immensely.'

He studied her as she spoke; her colour was heightened but her voice was firm. For some reason Stephen was glad she wasn't one of these blasé women who thought an exuberant use of eyelashes and an extra portion of charm would dupe him. 'Hmm! That's not a bad idea. I'd be reluctant to pull it down, my brother was a very enthusiastic player. I still use it occasionally.'

She secretly wondered with whom he played tennis. She smiled softly and said. 'To be honest, I'd like to move it, put it somewhere else, but you don't want too much change or expensive changes, so I left it.'

' . . . But the idea with the surround of trees etc. is OK . . . '

With his back to the windows, his face was in the shadows, but Sara could still see the energy and lively interest in his expression. She took the opportunity to further her ideas. 'I'm quite sure my plans will improve views from and of the house, without spoiling what is good and beautiful already. When you open the house to visitors, you'll need somewhere for them to stroll around, that's why I've suggested some new pathways. If you turn the kitchen garden into an old-fashioned herb garden, you can use it for outdoor receptions in the summer, and a retreat for visitors on windy days. Oh, I've used perennial flower everywhere.'

'Apart from the initial costs, what about the maintenance later? I don't want to have to employ extra gardeners; that would defeat my aims.'

Sara replied. 'You said you already have someone who cuts the lawns?'

He nodded. Looking at his face, she lost the thread of conversation for a moment.

He reminded her. ' . . . The cost of care and attention when you've finished?'

'Oh, yes! Sorry!' She swallowed her nerves and continued. 'When we leave, there won't be much to do for a while. Then, I suggest you get in a firm of gardeners to keep it under control once or twice a year, to do the cutting back, shaping, replacing. You'll be able to negotiate a good contract if you're prepared to leave it up to them when to fit it into their schedule. It doesn't really matter when they work, as long as they do it at the right time of year.'

'You'll notice I haven't included many flowerbeds, but a couple would make a great difference near the house. Perhaps there's a local pensioner who'd come in once or twice a week, to look after them?'

She was out of breath, and noticed an amused look on his face.

He shuffled the plans together. 'I'll look at these, and be in touch soon.'

Sara got to her feet, and straightened her skirt; it had slid up above her knees. He eyed the movement with interest, and came around the desk.

As he walked with her, back to the entrance, Sara was relaxed enough to ask. 'How old is the house?'

'An ancestor of mine was given the gift of the lands and the house for services to the crown, he pulled down the Tudor house that was on the site at the time, and built this one in the 1760's. It's been in the family ever since.'

'And now it's yours?'

His expression sobered. 'Yes. My older brother died a few years ago, and my father nine years ago. There's no-one else, and suddenly it's my responsibility.'

'I suppose that means you had to change your own plans?'

He nodded as they covered ground. 'Completely!'

'Did you mind?' She didn't look up at him, but was all ears.

'Very much, at first. but not any more. Now I only hope we can establish a controllable trust before my mother dies, if we don't, we might eventually go under because of the burden of inheritance tax.' He wondered why Sara Maxwell was making him talk so freely and reveal more than was absolutely necessary.

She nodded sympathetically. They reached the entrance door. She put out her hand. 'Thank you, Mr Dumont. I hope you like my suggestions, and if you have any questions, please get in touch. The office number is on the top of each plan.'

He mused that she barely reached his shoulder. There was something about her that he liked. He'd known a lot of women, and could usually pinpoint what he liked about them or not; he certainly didn't believe in romantic love — past experience had made him cynical. He was now forced into thinking about securing the future and about children to carry things on.

It would suffice though if he married someone like Lucy; that would be a comfortable, detached, and undemanding relationship. Stephen looked at Sara Maxwell speculatively before he shook her hand, and they went their separate ways.

2

He approved her plans and awarded *Designs and Possibilities* the commission. Sara heard through the grapevine there had been other companies bidding. She felt proud she'd managed to convince Stephen Dumont that they were the best choice! Since she started work at the beginning of the week, they'd moved from being 'Miss Maxwell' and 'Mr Dumont' to 'Stephen' and 'Sara' and she relaxed.

While examining the roots of some of the evergreens bordering the terrace to see if they had a chance to survive re-planting elsewhere, her mind was also busy estimating how best to accomplish all the work in the most efficient way. Sara was satisfied as she straightened up and looked around. She was going to order the trees and the other plants, bushes and flowers tomorrow.

She'd worked out a rough working schedule, and the workers were already busy with some of the preparatory work. There was a lot to do. Sara kept her room at the pub. The travelling distance from their main office would have made it impractical to be on site every day, but it was her first sole project and she wanted to be on the spot to monitor decisions, sort out problems, and to plan ahead. Brian understood that, and they agreed that he'd only pull her out of this job if there was a bottleneck or big problems elsewhere.

She noticed someone approaching, someone Sara had never seen before, but as she'd only been at Knowles House for a couple of days it wasn't surprising. She'd met the housekeeper, Mrs Booth; this was someone else. She was in her fifties, had a clear complexion, brown hair and pale grey eyes. She wore a fine tweed skirt and a lavender pullover and walked towards Sara with confidence.

'You must be Sara Maxwell? The garden specialist?' Her expression was friendly and open; her eyes were watchful and intelligent.

Sara smiled at her and nodded.

'I'm Marjorie Dumont, Stephen's mother.' She glanced down to where Sara had been digging around a rhododendron bush with a gardening trowel. 'Well, it's nice to see someone giving the garden attention at last. I tried to keep things going near the house . . . ' She held up her hands, ' . . . until these stopped me. It got too much for me, especially in the cold weather.'

Her hands had swollen joints. Sara asked sympathetically. 'Rheumatics?'

'Yes, and unfortunately chronic into the bargain. The garden was always too big for me, but I enjoyed doing as much as I could, as long as I could.' She shrugged. 'Still, lots of people are worse off than me; I shouldn't grumble. But I do miss pottering about, it was one of the few constructive things I could do.'

Sara threw back her head to let the wind blow her hair out of her eyes. 'You worked in the kitchen garden too, didn't you?'

Mrs Dumont nodded. 'I grew enough vegetables for our own use — lettuce, tomatoes, onions, etc., but most of the space was unused. The gardener used to dig it over for me, and blend in the manure.'

Comfortingly Sara said. 'But you can see someone cared. This flowerbed, and the potted plants on the terraces showed me someone was interested.'

The older woman nodded. 'But since the summer, I've had to give up, apart from the watering jobs!'

'If it's a comfort, the kitchen garden would be a wilderness now if you hadn't managed so long. It only needs a good clean up, and it'll look fine again.'

His mother smiled softly. 'It was my hobby. Stephen is too busy managing the estate, and he was never interested in gardening anyway. At least his plan to hire out the house means the gardens will get some care. I'm glad!'

Sara felt at ease with Marjorie Dumont. 'Will you mind, about strangers wandering round your home?'

She shrugged. 'We have to march with the times. It's better than having to sell out because there's too little income. Officially it's all in my name. Stephen asked me what I thought, I told him to go ahead and do whatever was necessary!'

'I promise that I'm not planning any sweeping changes — your son just wanted me to enhance things and add some colour. The garden is already lovely in its own way. It just needs some more focal points.'

'Stephen mentioned you asked who designed it in the first place. There are some old plans in the library; I think they must be the originals. They're a bit faded, but if you're still interested, I'll be glad to show them to you.'

Sara looked at the older woman with pleasure. 'That would be lovely — not that it makes any difference to what I'm doing now, I'm only interested for professional reasons.'

The lines deepened as Marjorie Dumont smiled. 'Why don't you come in for a cup of coffee, and then we'll go to the library upstairs, and I'll get them out.'

Sara looked down at her grimy jeans and mud-covered boots. 'I'm not dressed to walk around Knowles House, Mrs Dumont!'

Marjorie made a vague movement with her hand. 'Oh nonsense! Take off your boots, dust yourself down, and you'll be fine.'

Sara liked her uncomplicated attitude and smiled. 'Well . . . if you're sure?'

Mrs Dumont was already turning away. 'I'll put the kettle on; ready in five minutes! Come through the end window on the terrace. My husband and I had the rooms on this side of the house converted soon after we married. Stephen did the same to the rooms above, when he came back to take over.'

Ten minutes later Sara was sitting on

a towel spread on the seat of a comfortable chintz covered armchair and looking out on to the terrace. 'This is a lovely room, and what an inspirational view!'

'Yes, the house has very attractive ones from this side, hasn't it? That's why we chose this side and not the other; the tennis court blocks the best view over there. I still love watching the seasons. It's not just because of the colours, it's hard to explain; it has something to do with the atmosphere of the countryside, and the changing light.' She offered Sara a biscuit.

Sara refused with a slight shake of her head. She took a sip of the coffee. 'Umm! This is good! Wonderful when you've been outside for a while! Knowles House and the surrounding countryside is really beautiful Mrs Dumont. I understand why your son is determined to keep it in the family.'

'Please, call me Marjorie, everyone else does . . . Yes, I'm glad Stephen is trying to hang on; especially when he never reckoned it would be up to him. He didn't have a clue about running the estate, he only took a casual interest when he was young. My husband was there, and Darren was destined to carry on after him.'

Her forehead furrowed. 'Suddenly Stephen had to decide whether to take it on, or not. I think the fact that I was living here may have coloured his decision, but once he started to put his energy into learning about farming and herding and forestry and all the rest, he just ploughed ahead. He has a professional manager to help, but everyone tells me how much he's learned, and how fast.'

Sara absorbed the information with a nod. 'What did he do before?'

Marjorie took a sip of coffee. After a short pause she said. 'After university he went into banking, and apparently he was doing very well.' The sun from the windows locked some copper colour from Sara's hair. Marjorie liked her; she was an attractive woman, pleasant to talk to and interested in other people. A lot of young people these days only seemed interested in their friends and themselves.

'Banking knowledge will be vital to help him handle the financial side properly . . . if he's aiming to make the house a going concern. He . . . '

The door opened and the entrance of Stephen Dumont interrupted them; there was a young woman following at his heel.

Sara looked up. She'd spoken to Stephen several times about some aspect of the work since she arrived, and she thought it would be easy to keep up a professional attitude, but every time she saw him, she had the feeling that he was disturbing her sense of balance a little bit more.

He opened his mouth to say something and shut it when he saw her sitting with his mother. 'Oh! Hello, Sara! Having a coffee break? Mum, we just popped in to say Lucy and I are going into town. I have to pick up some contracts from the lawyers, and she thinks she's got to have a new dress, or die if she doesn't!'

The young woman moved closer to his side, and viewed Sara with interest. There was a smile on her face, but it didn't quite reach her eyes. 'Morning, Marjorie! He's exaggerating again! I can't wear the same thing to local events all the time, can I?' She paused. 'Stephen, what about introducing us?'

He hurried to oblige. 'Sara Maxwell — our garden designer.'

She looked at Sara's work-worn jeans, cheap anorak, and tousled hair in a banded red scarf. 'You take the job very seriously I see! Pleased to meet you!'

Sara buried a sense of annoyance and sensed that Lucy didn't view her with much friendliness. Lucy tucked her arm through his. It was a patent demonstration of her claims; Sara wondered why she bothered — Stephen Dumont's girlfriends were none of her business. Sara responded with a nod and 'Hello!'

Marjorie Dumont smiled up at them. 'Want a cup of coffee before you go?'

Stephen replied. 'No, I just wondered if you needed anything?'

'Nothing that can't wait till I go myself, but thanks anyway! I'm going to show Sara the plans for the garden.'

Sara took a sip of coffee. Lucy was an extremely attractive, well-groomed young woman with blonde, almost white hair fixed with two tortoiseshell clips loosely behind her ears. She had bright blue eyes, delicate features and a sylphlike figure in designer clothes. Sara wished she looked tidier — at the moment she looked like a farm labourer.

She shook her thoughts, she'd gone through a long training to learn how to make something beautiful out of nothing, Lucy had probably never done anything physical in her whole life. Sara's hand shook a little as she replaced the cup in the saucer. She stared silently out of the windows, and listened as the others talked about someone they knew. Eventually, she echoed Marjorie Dumont's, 'Bye!' when Stephen and Lucy left.

Marjorie explained. 'Lucy comes from the next farm to ours. She and Stephen have known each other since childhood.'

Sara nodded without comment and leaned forward to accept another coffee.

Bent over the old documents, she was fascinated. 'Good heavens! The oak trees are originals; they're in exactly the same place today. I knew they were old, but the only way to really find out is to axe them.'

Amused by her enthusiasm, Marjorie smiled. 'Yes, it's interesting, isn't it? Living history!'

Sara's voice grew excited as she pointed at the chart. 'There used to be a sunken garden in front of the terrace. Look! The terrace led down to a paved pathway and from there down two or three steps, into a small formal garden.'

Marjorie looked over her shoulder at

the drawings. 'Hmm! Yes, is that what it's supposed to be?' She grew silent for a minute. 'Do you know something? I think there are parts of it still there! Unless I'm mistaken, there's stonework under the rhododendrons opposite the terrace steps. I often wondered what they were!'

Sara's eyes widened. 'Really? That would be a fantastic find! I wonder why it was covered in?' Sara examined and commented on the drawings for a while, but her thoughts were elsewhere. She looked up. 'Marjorie, I'm bursting with curiosity about that stonework!'

Marjorie laughed. 'I can see! I thought you might like to see the rest of the house, but it can wait for another day.'

She followed Sara downstairs, and they went outside together. She showed Sara the stonework under some rhododendrons. Sara's excitement grew as she kneeled; scraping some earth she found the stonework seemed to curve gently. If her guess was right, it was the top of the balustrades leading down to the sunken garden. The garden had either been destroyed when the ground was filled to the height of the gravel walk, or it had been left intact, just filled in and was waiting to be rediscovered. Sara hoped for the second.

Digging away next morning, she decided the balustrade was probably intact. It was hard work, because roots made progress difficult.

Marjorie came out to check up. 'How will you know if the rest is there?'

'The simplest test would be to drill a hole down as far as the pathway. We have the measurements of where it was, and we should hit stone if it's still there.'

'And if you find it? What then?'

'Then I have to persuade Stephen to let me expose it, and somehow I don't think he likes to hear about anything that costs extra money!'

'No, you're right there!' Marjorie laughed. 'But wouldn't it be great to have something so original next to the house again!'

Sara grinned. 'Wonderful! How can I persuade him?'

'You can't; he has to be convinced himself. The only way is to present the facts and don't beat about the bush; he likes things to be straightforward. I can support you, but he makes the decisions.'

'It would be so frustrating if it's there and he turns it down! I'm almost tempted to say I'll do it for nothing!'

'Don't you dare! Moving all that earth is definitely no job for a woman.'

Sara laughed. 'I wasn't actually thinking of doing it by hand!' She sighed. 'It's a chance in a million!'

She was sure it was there. She sorted out what she would say in her mind, and made her way to the estate office. Alan Harris, the estate manager, was busy checking some milking records, but he shoved them aside when she came in and made them some coffee.

They'd chatted before a couple of times when they'd bumped into each other, and Sara decided he was a nice person. He had friendly blue eyes, light brown hair that was usually out of control, and a tall, slim figure. She asked how he'd come to be manager at Knowles House. Handling his mug and taking the occasional sip, he told her where he came from, and how he'd seen the advert in a national newspaper.

'It was the first time I had an interview with someone who knew less about farming than I did. I think Steve took me on instinct, he didn't know enough in those days to judge how knowledgeable I was. He's learned a lot though, and nowadays he's very competent but still wants me to tell him if I think he's off course. I admire how he's learned the ropes in such a short time.'

'What happens when he knows it all? Do you lose your job?'

'No, I'll continue to handle the estate's day-to-day business, and he'll have more time to concentrate on running things like this scheme for special events at the house, checking up on me, and establishing other things he has in the pipeline.'

Sara nodded and took a sip. 'Who's handling the catering, flower displays, etc, when this scheme takes off? His mother?'

Alan shook his head. 'As far as I know he's going to use outside firms for that sort of thing. I think he wants to keep pressure off his mother. She hadn't really got over her husband's death, when Stephen's brother died; it knocked her sideways. Perhaps he's planning to hand it over to Lucy when they marry. Have you met her?'

Sara didn't like the idea as it flitted though her brain, but she nodded. 'I didn't know they were getting married. Yes, I met her once, at the house.'

'Oh, it's nothing official yet, purely supposition, but every one assumes that's where it's heading. They've known each other since the cradle. Her father owns neighbouring land, and she has all it takes to run a stately home to a T.'

She looked down at her mug and changed the subject. 'What about you, Alan? Are you married?'

'No. I haven't had time to look for a wife. You're not looking for Mr Right by any chance are you? You're not wearing any rings!'

She gave a throaty chuckle. Sara liked him. He had a kind face. She judged him to be in his late thirties.

They were both still laughing when Stephen Dumont opened the door and came in. He eyed them for a second or so. 'Hello, Sara! Got a problem?'

'Yes, can you spare a few minutes?'

Alan got up and picked up a pile of milking records. 'I'm off to Top Farm with these, I promised Joe to work out his averages so that he can compare the yield with his feeding. Bye, Sara! Perhaps I'll see you down the pub one evening?'

She coloured; Stephen's eyes never left her face. 'Yes . . . by all means!'

Alan startled to whistle as he made his way out of the door and across the yard. The sound of it echoed back to the office.

'So, what did you want to talk about?'

Was it her imagination, or did his voice have a slight edge. Sara swallowed her nervousness, and hoped that she hadn't picked a bad moment to ask him. She told him briefly about the garden, and what would be involved in exposing it.

He studied her face as she spoke, and remained silent until she finished. 'You know this isn't part of the financial plan you made! It would be an expensive undertaking. It is not necessary, is it?' His words were cool; their meaning was as clear as ice water.

'It's not 'necessary', but it's advisable.' Her voice sounded stiff and unnatural. 'I can't imagine why it was filled in; it was part of the original house. It would increase the optical worth of the house on that side immensely, and is also a windfall from the historical viewpoint. It would also provide a perfect walking area for visitors.

'I suggested making pathways elsewhere in the garden, but you could forget them if you have this garden. We could provide some additional benches elsewhere in the garden for anyone who wants to wander further afield. A sunken garden near the house would be enough for most visitors.'

His eyes swept over her. 'So there'll be no additional expense? Is that what you're saying?'

'I'm not saying anything of the sort!' Her tawny eyes flashed in brief irritation. 'Of course it will cost more. There's a lot of earth to move, and the land will have to be levelled and realigned afterwards.'

He turned towards the coffee machine and picked up a mug. 'Then forget it! There's not even a definite guarantee that if it is there, that it's not damaged.'

Illogically, Sara wondered why she'd made the effort to put on make-up this morning, just because she knew she'd be seeing him. She managed to reply through stiff lips. 'Then I hope you'll understand when I say that I think you're wrong. If you dismiss outright this chance to do something special for your house, then your commitment isn't as strong as I thought it was.' She knew she was going beyond the bounds of her job, but it didn't stop her. 'Knowles House deserves that garden! You're just rejecting it outright!'

The line of his mouth tightened a fraction, and he eyed her steadily. 'I've no bones to pick with your work so far, but I'll remind you it's not your concern what I decide to do. If you can prove the costs won't be exorbitant, I might give it second thoughts.'

He poured himself coffee and looked at her again. 'Is there anything else?'

Her heart sank and she bit her lip in dismay. 'No. That was it.' Her mind and body began to function together again. He was right; it was his decision.

'Good, then I suggest we both get back to our work! When you know how much it would actually cost, drop the figures into the office, and I'll let you know.'

3

Sara did a costing analysis and put it on his desk in the estate office, going there after she'd just seen him speeding down the drive. If he decided against it, she didn't want to hear it from him direct on the spot or face those dark eyes. She almost wished she'd never suggested looking for the garden in the first place.

When she reflected on their conversation she had a stupid feeling of disappointment. She knew it was silly to give it a second thought; he was her employer, and she'd learned to accept that people didn't always welcome her suggestions. But this time, no matter how much she tried to ignore it, the idea that Stephen Dumont didn't agree with her point of view bothered her more than she cared to admit.

One morning when she was marking positions for trees, Marjorie came across the stretch of open grass to ask her how Stephen had reacted to her news.

Sara told her; his mother wasn't surprised. She smiled understandingly. 'Don't give up hope. He might still come round, when he's had time to think about it, and as long as it doesn't cost too much.'

Sara swallowed as she remembered her calculations, and her hopes took another downward turn. She hunched her shoulders, shrugged, and dug her hands deeper into her pocket. 'Isn't there a saying; that hope dies last?'

Sara forced herself to concentrate on the rest of the work. Some of the plants and shrubs she'd ordered were beginning to arrive, and she wanted them planted as soon as possible.

Unnoticed by her, Stephen walked across the open ground and came to join her, his footsteps were silenced by the soft grass. The light breezes blew his dark hair askew and his eyes narrowed as his attention fixed on her slight figure as he quickly approached with long strides.

He sat down nearby on a conveniently fallen log. A slow smile covered his face and something flamed in his eyes. Sara stood up holding the bush awkwardly in position, while pressing the soft earth firmly into place with her foot. She stepped back to view her work, resting on the shaft of the spade.

'Perfect!'

His voice made her jump, and she spun around. 'Heavens, Stephen! How long have you been there? You gave me a fright!'

Exertion had heightened the colour in her cheeks, the fresh breezes had blown her hair completely haywire, and her tawny eyes were glowing with the satisfaction of a job well done.

'Did I? I've been here a few minutes.' With tongue in cheek he continued. 'I was content to sit and watch you; and I didn't want to interrupt the work. It's my lord-of-the-manor neurosis, I expect!' He paused and took in the picture of Sara with the spread of the hillside in the background. 'Actually I did have a sensible reason to look for you; I came to tell you to go ahead and search for the garden! I'm probably going to regret it, but my mother is just excited about it, and with two resolute women on my back I've decided to surrender!'

Sara's face split into a smile of sheer delight and let the spade fall. 'Oh that's great! I have a feeling you won't regret it — honestly!'

He tilted his head to the side. 'I hope so. After all it is only speculation, and I don't need to tell you it's a lot of money to throw to the wind if it turns out to be a wild-goose chase!!'

She felt so happy, it showed in her expression, and suddenly Stephen didn't think about the money any more.

She was a little breathless as she insisted, 'It's there; everything points to it. We tested for stonework in several places and hit it.'

Sara covered the distance between

them quickly, and threw herself down uninvited next to him. Unexpectedly he felt pleased with himself and the world in general. He gave her a brief glance and looked into the distance. 'Let's hope so.'

Sara followed the direction of his eyes, and studied the surrounding landscape. She took off her thick working gloves and slapped them against her thighs. 'Knowles House, and the estate is lovely. The longer I'm here, the more I like it; the fold of the hills, the colour of the fields and woods, the blue-grey mist when it rises from the river first thing in the morning. There's a subtle change and something new to see every day. I know it's a financial burden for you, but it's a jewel!'

He leaned forward and rested his arms on his thighs. 'Yes, I agree. The woods are covered in a thick carpet of bluebells in the spring. It's incredible; the blue covering is almost out of this world. I think Van Gogh would have loved putting it on canvas. The grass in the low meadows is so lush and green in springtime, and the crops fill the fields with gold in the autumn.

'I've been told there are even endangered species of flowers growing along the banks of the river at the bottom of that field over there.'

He pointed, and her eyes followed the direction. 'It's my home and of course I think it's a special place, but I'm glad you seem to like it too. Sometimes I wish there wasn't so much work and responsibility to keep it all intact, but that's how things go, the only alternative is not to care and sell it off piece-by-piece. Who knows what the district would look like then in fifty years' time. No more bluebells, another sprawling suburban estate up in the grazing fields, and just one smallholding left . . . ' He absentmindedly picked up a twig and opened his mouth. 'It doesn't bear . . . ' He cut short, and turned towards the sound of hoofs.

A rider astride a grey hunter

approached swiftly; it was Lucy. She pulled up her horse to a practiced stop. Her blonde hair, drawn back out of sight, hidden under her riding cap; her riding jacket and jodhpurs fitted like a second skin and her black riding boots emphasised her shapely legs.

She eyed them intensely. 'Hi, Stephen! I've been looking for you.' She managed to give Sara a brief nod. 'Alan told me you were looking for Sara, so I came to get you.'

Stephen looked up; she was controlling the nervous prancing of the horse with practiced ease. He eyed her speculatively. 'What for? Something special?'

'You never said if you're coming to Charlie Orsmann's dinner party on Friday, or not!' She noticed his expression and hesitation. 'I thought so, you've forgotten, haven't you? Charlie is a stickler for equal male and females; if you can't come I'll have to find someone else! I promised to let him know tonight.'

Stephen ran his fingers through his hair; it fell back obediently into place. 'Charlie? Oh, yes! True you did mention it; and I had forgotten! OK, I'll come!'

Lucy nodded with satisfaction and threw one leg elegantly over the saddle and slid gracefully to the ground. With the reins gripped firmly in one hand, she said, 'I'll walk back to the house with you. Your mother is making us tea, so come on!' She put out her free gloved hand, and he had little choice but to take it and stand up.

Sara got up too. She put her working gloves on again and walked towards the fallen spade to pick it up. Stephen's voice drifted over her shoulder.

'You'll sort everything out, Sara, and let me know? About the digging?'

Sara nodded. 'Yes, of course. I'll get in touch with my boss today and find out when we can have the small excavator and a lorry for a couple of days.'

'Digging? What for?' Lucy hassled

Stephen to explain. She clapped her hands together when he did. 'How exciting! The perfect addition to Knowles House! I always thought the garden needed a focal point. Lawns everywhere are a bit boring, darling! I do hope Sara finds it. We must give a party if she does.'

Sara didn't miss the 'we' and she swallowed a sense of loss, although she realised it was silly. She didn't belong here, and had no claims on Stephen Dumont.

★　★　★

Sara felt dirty; in fact she felt very filthy. She'd been cleaning the stonework of the rediscovered pathway with a high-pressure hose. She switched off the cleaner and stood back to survey her work. The garden, with its formal pathway was free. The stone slabs and central feature looked fairly clean. There were some small repairs, a couple of slab-stones would have to be replaced, and the attractive stonework bowl had to be reattached to the central feature, but the recovery process had gone well. The surrounding bank-work had been secured and made ready for planting.

Their truck had transported the earth to a corner of the garden, where Sara decided to make a large circular rockery. The rest of her team had left long ago. The foreman had offered to stay and finish the job with her, but Sara had sent him home. She looked up at the darkening sky, there were rain clouds massing over by the woodlands.

Pools of shadows on the grass were already scrambling to find their way up to the terrace via the gravel pathway. The silhouette of the house was gradually merging into the surrounding darkness, and although some light spilled out from Mrs Dumont's rooms and there was still some daylight, the house was settling down for the night to be wrapped up in a cocoon of silence and obscurity.

Sara stretched her aching back and started to remove the yellow oilskin dungarees, dancing from one foot to the other to do so. She heard footsteps, and her heart skipped a beat; her senses heightened when she saw it was Stephen.

Standing in front of her, most of his face lost in the shadows, he declared. 'I've seen you covered in dirt before, but never as bad as this!'

She looked up at him and smiled softly. Her teeth sparkled white in her mud-splattered face. 'I bet! But it's all part of the job.'

He tilted his head. 'Do you really have to get so involved yourself?'

She shrugged her shoulders, gave him a wry smile, and folded the dripping canary yellow overalls neatly over her arm. Her jeans and pullover had wet patches, water had got inside her wellingtons, and she knew her hair was hanging in rats' tails. 'No. I could stand back and watch someone else do it. It may seem odd to you, but I actually enjoy doing it, and as I was the one who started things off, I wanted to see it through myself.'

He stuck his thumbs in the pockets of his chinos, and studied her face for a moment. 'I'm thinking about going out for a meal. I don't feel like cooking this evening. You deserve a special treat; would you like to come?'

She was more surprised than she showed. 'With you?'

He looked pointedly right and left. 'Is there anyone else around?'

Her heart flip-flopped and she looked down. In control again a moment later, she met his dark eyes and said, 'Looking like this?'

His reply was laced with dry amusement. 'To be perfectly honest, I did hope you'd clean yourself up first.'

'How much time do I have?'

Stephen gazed at her. 'I'll pick you up at half-seven.'

A few minutes ago Sara had felt dog-tired; her only thoughts had been a hot bath, and a warm bed. Now she was wound up like a small child on Christmas Eve. She reminded herself that even though the offer was special to her, it was an unexceptional move for him. He was being a considerate employer; giving her a reward. Perhaps he just didn't like eating on his own. 'No, the worst of the work is finished.'

Marjorie Dumont was about to draw the curtains and automatically looked out of the sitting room window. She saw Sara and Stephen standing and talking. She paused for a moment clutching the thick damask drapes in her hands. She viewed them with interest; their dark silhouettes were so close together they fired her imagination with speculations.

She shook her head softly, no, that was silly. She liked Sara very much, but Stephen wasn't likely to rush headlong into a meaningless affair with someone who would be gone in a couple of weeks. She'd adjusted to the idea that Stephen and Lucy would take over Knowles House one day.

Lucy and Stephen had grown up

together and she would sail elegantly and without a hitch into the position of his wife and hostess. If Stephen loved Lucy, then it would work out fine. If Stephen married Lucy because he thought she was right, without really loving her, then he would end up miserable, and that was too high a price to pay. She could only hope that he didn't disregard his own feelings whatever he decided. Marjorie knew she'd have no say in it. He'd go his own way.

Why had life worked out like it had? Jack had been ill for a long time before he died, and although never a day passed without her thinking about him, somehow she'd come to terms with that.

Darren's death was harder to accept. While driving too fast round a narrow bend in the road, he'd collided head on with an oncoming tractor, and was killed on the spot. All the polite words of comfort, suggestions and reassurance from everyone didn't help. She was still going down a dark tunnel with just a tiny pinpoint of light ahead.

She closed the curtains with a practiced swish of the material, and went to turn on the television.

The muted light in the hallway was a poor source of illumination. The wife of the pub owner was on her way from the kitchen to the public bar, when the tinny doorbell rang. She broke into a wide smile when she opened the side door to Stephen. 'Well, Mr Dumont! We haven't seen you for ages. How's your mother?'

'Fine! I've been busy but I don't intend to desert you for ever Elsie!'

'I should hope not!' The pub owner's wife smiled up at him. 'Can I help you? Need something special? You don't usually come to the side entrance.'

'I'm picking someone up.' Any other explanations were unnecessary; Sara came hurrying down the staircase towards him.

'Am I late?'

He eyed her stylish figure in a tweed skirt and soft ivory pullover. There was a short camelhair coat slung casually over her shoulders. 'No, dead on time!'

Saying goodbye to Elsie, they left; Stephen following her out.

Elsie raised her eyebrows as she watched them leave and hurried off down the corridor to tell her husband that Master Stephen from Knowles House and their guest from upstairs were out together, would you believe it!

Sara got into his BMW parked opposite. She felt a little tense, but was determined to put any doubt and questions, aside. His invitation was innocent, and she'd just enjoy it. He'd asked her to share an evening meal, not his life. Even if he was getting engaged to Lucy, officially he was still free, so she wasn't grabbing someone else's property.

'We're going to a small restaurant I know near Westbury.' He was driving competently, and when he spoke, he turned his head slightly towards her.

She said cheerfully, 'I could eat a horse.'

He laughed. 'I'm not surprised! Do you always work so hard?'

'It depends on the job; but it improves my standing with the workers no end.' Autumn was approaching fast; Sara noticed some leaves were already floating to the ground as the gusts of wind shook the trees.

'I hope you realise it was a chance in a million to find your garden still intact? I wonder why they didn't demolish it?'

'Why demolish it, if it was all going to be covered and levelled out anyway?'

'Yes, I suppose you're right! I'll give the stone surfaces a good going over with some special cleaning liquid, but it's still in remarkably good condition. What does your mother think?'

'She's cock-a-hoop, and keeps reminding me I almost missed the chance! You can already see its shape and the size from her living room window.' He gave her a reluctant smile. 'I must admit; it's a great addition to Knowles House.'

He wasn't someone who smiled often; it was something Sara had noticed about him. But his smiles, when they came, were all the more valuable. She needed to reassure him. 'I know that it was an unexpected expense, but it'll be worth every penny; promise! Wait until it's been planted, and the central feature is back in place. It's an authentic part of the house's history; I'm certain people will love strolling around there when they visit!'

He looked across briefly. 'You'd make good legal advocate, Sara. I think if you made up your mind, you could persuade the devil to be good.'

She coloured in the darkness. 'And I'm sure you wouldn't have agreed to anything, unless you were convinced it was the right thing to do!'

★ ★ ★

The food tasted wonderful; the minestrone was full of tasty fresh vegetables, the scaloppini and risotto were perfect, and the dessert of pieces of fresh fruit, partly dipped in chocolate rounded off a great meal. Perhaps she enjoyed it because she was very hungry, or the atmosphere of the small room with its red-checked tablecloths, candles in Chianti bottles, and soft music was so attractive, or because she was with someone she liked.

The waitress cleared the table and they dallied over their wine. Stephen had rationed himself to one glass, because of driving. Sara almost wished the evening would never end. There were no awkward moments of silence, or forced conversation. She was pleased they had a lot in common. He was an interesting man, who was easy to talk to.

The return journey flew. Back at the pub, Sara turned to him in the darkness of the car. 'Thanks, Stephen, for a lovely meal.'

Stephen got out of the car and came around. She got out. The street lighting formed a halo around her head. 'My pleasure! I enjoyed it too. Tired?'

She wondered if he was thinking

about asking her into the bar for a farewell drink. 'A bit; I'll sleep well tonight.'

He watched her curiously. They were close, and he leaned slightly towards her. The pub door opened, and Stephen straightened. A man passed them and said, 'Goodnight!' Stephen answered him but Sara barely registered when he passed. Had it just been a figment of her imagination or just wishful thinking that Stephen was going to kiss her? Sara made an effort to sound natural. 'Goodnight!'

'Goodnight, Sara'

Sara dashed upstairs, closed the door, and leaning against it was lost in thoughts.

Stephen sat staring ahead for a short time before he started the engine. He didn't need any extra complications in his life, but admittedly, he liked her.

He didn't notice the curtains moving slightly as Sara took a last peek.

4

It was a fine Friday afternoon. The streets were busy, and people were on the go, Sara was shopping in the nearby market town. She'd decided to travel home tomorrow to visit her parents, check up on her flat and sort out any personal correspondence, instead of going this afternoon. She'd also arranged to meet Brian on Monday morning, to inform him about progress before she returned to Knowles on Monday evening. She felt little urge to go home; although usually she looked forward to catching up on family news, contacting friends, and going out with one of them.

Meandering through a well-stocked branch of Boots, filling her shopping basket with various cosmetics and other necessities, she felt glad to be dressed in something other than jeans, dungarees, or weatherproofs. Pale linen trousers, a matching lightweight jacket, and a silk shirt in aquamarine, gave her a feeling of being fashionably chic for once.

'Sara! It is Sara, isn't it? Good heavens, you do look different when you're dressed in something decent!'

Sara looked up. 'Oh! Lucy. Hello!' Lucy's supple young body was in a designer suit, the colour of lapis lazuli. Today her hair was fixed in a classic austere chignon. More than one man gave her an admiring glance, and although Sara didn't realise it, they were admiring her too.

'I was just about to go for coffee. I've been looking for a pair of shoes for an outfit I'm wearing at a reception next week, but of course the shops here have nothing suitable. I had a feeling it would be a waste of time but it was worth a try. I'll have to go up to London to find something on Monday now. Feel like a coffee?'

There was no reason to refuse. It was offered in a friendly way, and a cup of coffee would be welcome. 'Yes, why not?'

She nodded and gave Sara a good-humoured smile. 'Good! I hate drinking coffee on my own. Let's go to Angelo's, he has a small terrace out the back.'

They were seated at a small bistro table. Sunlight filled the terrace; the air was fresh, loaded with the heavenly aroma of fresh brewed coffee.

Sara looked around approvingly. 'This is nice. You'd never suspect there was anywhere like this out the back.'

'Strangers or tourists wouldn't, but local people know.'

That put Sara in her place.

Lucy motioned the waitress who was passing on her way to another customer with a lifted hand. 'One espresso and . . . ?' She looked at Sara expectantly.

Sara said 'Cappuccino.'

' . . . and a cappuccino.' Lucy settled back in her chair as the waitress moved on. 'I hear you've finished excavating the garden? Stephen is delighted, and Marjorie is euphoric. What a lucky find!'

'Yes, isn't it? I've spent most of this week finishing the cleaning work. It looks quite good already and after I've planted shrubs and plants next week, it'll be beyond compare.'

'I can't say I'd like to do your job; all that dirt under the fingernails all the time!'

The waitress returned with their order.

Sara shrugged. 'There are gloves, and nailbrushes and hand-cream. But if you don't like gardening, I suppose nothing helps, you'll always hate it. There's a lot of dirt and work behind a beautiful garden.'

Lucy took a neat sip from the small espresso cup. Her professionally manicured nails and fingers replaced it in the saucer. 'Don't get the wrong idea, I love flowers, I just don't fancy all the work involved.'

Sara wondered what Lucy did with

her time. 'What do you do?'

The cornflower blue eyes had a resolute set to them. 'You mean work? I went to a secretarial college in London, to please my father, but I couldn't face the prospect of a nine-to-five job in a pokey office, so I came home. I help him arrange events on the estate. I'm a committee member of some of the local charities, and . . . oh, you know that sort of thing! I've plenty to keep me busy.'

Sara had the urge to remark that daughters of well-to-do families were doing exactly the same a hundred years ago, but women had moved on since then, but she didn't. 'Oh, I see! And your mother encourages you? Doesn't she want you to have your own income, be independent, that sort of thing?'

'My mother left Daddy when I was a teenager. I don't see her anymore; it would upset Daddy if I did. Sometimes you have to make difficult choices! Daddy is very generous with money so there is no need for me to actually work.'

She paused and asked casually, 'Did you enjoy the meal with Stephen in Westbury the other night?'

Sara's colour heightened a little. So Lucy knew, either from Stephen himself, or someone else had seen them and told her. 'Yes, it was very nice.'

'It's typical of Stephen! He is very considerate to his employees. Daddy often says he's too thoughtful; that he should keep a tight rein on, to avoid anyone taking advantage.'

Sara hooked the cup and took another sip to give her hands something to do. 'You don't honestly believe anyone can take advantage of Stephen against his will, do you?'

Lucy's laugh had a hollow tone. 'All men are slightly hopeless at judging people's true characters. Stephen is a dear, but he doesn't always think about the long-term effect of being too friendly.' She reached out and brushed Sara's arm softly. 'I don't mean he shouldn't have shown gratitude for a job well done in your case, of course!' She gave Sara a sickening smile. 'I just think he sometimes gives people the wrong impression, that's all.'

Sara's hackles were rising. 'All the people I've met here like and respect him. No-one thinks he's a pushover or an easy target. He's taken on a difficult job, and the people on the estate and hereabout are all behind him.'

Lucy's eyebrows rose and she looked perplexed.

Sara steamed ahead. 'Taking over from his brother must have been very hard, especially when he had completely different plans for his life.'

Lucy's voice had a slight drawl and she sounded impatient. 'Of course! I agree completely, but he should be careful when he chooses his friends and acquaintances. The family at Knowles House have always had an important central role to play. Stephen needs to watch his position . . . '

Sara's irritation was growing. 'Lucy,

the role of the lord of the manor went out with the dodo! Stephen needs to run the estate as a going concern, he needs to be a business manager, his social skills or his standing in modern society is of secondary importance. He wants to retain Knowles House but he'll have to work damned hard to do that. Ask anyone who still owns a stately home — they'll bend your ears telling you how much effort they have to put into keeping it in the family. Nowadays the treasure chests are empty, the working forces are liberated, and no-one cares what the landed gentry think any more!'

Lucy flushed. 'I think you underestimate the role of local society.'

'What do you mean exactly? Are you talking about money, about class distinction, about behaviour or about people's opinion? I think you're out of touch; achievement and performance is what matters today.'

Sara stopped mid-sentence and steadied her thoughts. 'But, let's not argue about it.' She looked at her watch. 'I still have a lot to do.' It wasn't true, she'd already finished her shopping, but she'd had enough of Lucy's company for one day. She picked up her bags. 'It was nice to see you, Lucy. Hope you're lucky and find those shoes when you get to London!'

Lucy viewed her with a strained expression and gave her a stiff smile. 'Yes, so do I.'

★   ★   ★

Sara had been trailing behind Marjorie Dumont on a tour of the house. The rooms were beautiful and all the ones she saw had high ornate ceilings. They were skilfully furnished with antiques that had been in the family for generations.

Upstairs the ballroom ran three-quarters of the length of one side of the house. Gold, white and yellow dominated the room. The gold and white plasterwork high above them was intricate and elaborate, the long mirrors reflected the light from the paned windows opposite, and the huge fireplace in the middle had a light marble surround with a mounted mirror.

The floor was of highly polished toffee coloured wood with inlaid patterns in a darker shade. Ornate candelabras hung from the ceiling and there were also some standing candelabras alongside elegant sofas dotted down the whole length of the walls.

'What a fantastic room! I can just imagine the balls and celebrations that took place here through the centuries!'

Marjorie looked around. 'Yes, it is lovely isn't it? As far as I know it hasn't been used regularly as a ballroom since the beginning of the Second World War. We did have a reception and dance here when I married Stephen's father, that's the only time I can remember it in use. I'll never forget that of course.'

'What a pity that this room has been damned to perpetual silence, and what a waste of space! It must be a nightmare to keep clean — all the gilt, and plasterwork,' Sara said.

'Some women from the village come up once a week. They usually take on one or two rooms at a time. They're the people who keep the house alive by opening windows, chasing the dust, renewing the polish, removing the cobwebs, cleaning the windows, but no-one lives in these rooms anymore and that's very sad. The plasterwork has to be cleaned by specialist firms using scaffolding as a platform.

'We try to rotate things so that each room gets a thorough cleaning now and then, but it's an expensive task that gets even more expensive with the passing years. I can't do much to help any more. The rooms are totally impractical living quarters by modern-day standards.'

They wandered out, and along the corridor into the next room, which turned out be a ladies' sitting room, with pale-green silk wallpaper, and some lovely furniture. A sewing table with boxwood inlay stood in front of the window, an eight-day long-case clock stood in one corner, and some elegant chairs and a matching couch stood facing the veined marble fire-place.

Sara looked around. 'I can understand why Stephen is hiring it out; if he doesn't, these rooms will never have any real purpose any more, will they?'

'No, but I think he'll keep a close tag on things for a while. If things get too damaged, he'll reverse his decision. I don't think he'll put up with people ruining the place however much money comes in.'

Sara looked thoughtful. 'It will take a lot of organisation and control, but I'm sure he's already thought about that.'

A connecting door led from that room into one of the main bedrooms. A mahogany chest-on-chest in rich brown tones stood next to one wall, near it on the wall was an oil portrait of a middle-aged woman sitting at a table.

She had a white frilled bonnet on her head, and black button eyes dominated the lively expression in her face. A tall backed walnut wing chair at the foot of the bed was upholstered in dark green, and a window seat was placed strategically in the window niche. Fine side tables displayed some Chinese figures, and a bracket clock. Sara looked up at the portrait.

'Who was she?'

'She's a family member, rather notorious so it seems. She wasn't aristocracy, wasn't even a member of the landed gentry, and that was a dreadful shortcoming in those days of course. She was the daughter of a sea captain. She travelled with her father everywhere after the death of her mother, and on a voyage to India one of the Dumont men fell hopelessly in love with her.'

'They married in secret. It wouldn't have upset the family so much, if his older brother hadn't been killed at Waterloo. Suddenly her husband was the heir to the estate.'

Sara took a closer look at the picture.

'You can tell she must have been beautiful when she was young.'

'There is a smaller picture of her in Stephen's room downstairs, painted when she was nineteen. She was really beautiful, and hot-headed, and unteachable. She refused to conform to convention, treated the servants as equals, and ignored social etiquette. Her husband had a sticky time of it with his contemporaries, but a wonderful life with her, so it seems. She said what she thought, and often called one of their guests a 'doddering old fool', or a 'cackling old busybody'. That was social suicide in those days of course!'

Sara laughed. 'Definitely not the best way to make friends and influence people, but she must have been an interesting woman.'

'Today we'd have labelled her as a radical and I'm not really sure if she and I would have got on, but I do admire women who have fire in their bellies and get things done. People put pressure on him to divorce her but he wouldn't consider it, or of throwing her out. He loved her too much.'

'What a romantic story. She sounds like an intriguing woman. Did they have any children?'

'Eleven! And all of them made it to adulthood. She took charge of the nursery and their early education. Something that also shocked her contemporaries, because the upper classes in those days fobbed their babies and children off on to other women.'

Sara tilted her head to the side. 'Do you know something? I almost feel sorry for her husband. It sounds like she was a strong personality who steamrolled everyone in her path.'

Marjorie answered spontaneously. 'Well they had eleven children, so he wasn't steamrolled for long, was he?'

They eyed each other for a moment silently and broke into simultaneous peals of laughter. The corridor door opened and Stephen stuck his head around it. He looked at them and said, 'I wondered who was in here.' He followed the direction of their eyes and looked up at the portrait. 'What's the joke?'

The two women paused, looked up, at each other, and then started laughing again. He gave them a puzzled look, shook his head, and closed the door. Outside a slow smile spread across his face before he went on his way.

5

Sara decided to stay in the village the following weekend instead of going home. She wanted to catch up with the paperwork.

After sorting neat piles of paper into orders, delivery notes, and other categories across the surface of the chintz bedspread in her room at the pub, she sat down at the small writing desk in front of the window with her notebook and set to work. Now and then her eyes were drawn to the road running through the village. It was a bright Saturday morning, full of sunshine, and people were busy with their weekend preparations.

Looking longingly, beyond the fields opposite towards the woodland where the edges of the leaves were telling of the imminent arrival of autumn, she promised herself a walk as soon as she was finished. The thought spurred her on to work faster.

'Drat!' She spoke to a silent, empty room. She could see that some of the measurements in one of her sketches were wrong; the kitchen garden wasn't a long narrow strip like noted. She'd have to measure it properly; she wanted to order paving stones for a dry area around the glasshouse entrance. She grabbed her car keys, and a soft leather jacket — the tan shade complimented her hair and eyes.

A couple of minutes later she drove through the open entrance gates of Knowles House. She changed into her wellingtons, took an ultrasonic distance meter and a writing pad from the box of things she always had in the boot of her car, and set off towards the kitchen garden.

The house and garden looked lovely in the morning light. The folds of the hills in the distance were still covered in a thin misty veil. The silence everywhere was a balm for the soul, and the air was fresh and clean after some light showers the previous night.

A little time later, Marjorie found her near the glasshouse at the far end of the kitchen garden. Sara was sitting on a convenient rock, noting down the measurements she'd just taken; she looked up and smiled at the older woman.

'Good heavens Sara, what are you doing here? Are you addicted to your work? Do you never stop?'

Sara laughed softly and pushed her hair into place behind her ears. 'Of course I do! But I tend to ignore the paperwork for as long as I can. Eventually I have to do it, it's part of my job. I decided I'd do it this weekend, but found I'd some wrong measurements of the kitchen garden. I'm remeasuring it.'

'I thought you always went home at the weekend?'

'I do, but not this weekend.' Sara gestured in the direction of the glasshouse. 'The glasshouse isn't in a bad shape, is it? Wouldn't it be an idea to use it for storing plants and flowers for arrangements in the house, when things take off?'

'Hmm! I don't think Stephen will exactly jump for joy if he has to pay someone to look after plants in the glasshouse, he'll probably leave that sort of thing to the local flower shop.'

Sara looked at the tip of her wellingtons and hoped she wasn't going too far. 'Sophisticated flower arrangements for special events need to be done by a professional, but what about the odd vase of flowers here and there just to make the house attractive and homely?' Sara could see Marjorie was curious, so she ploughed on. 'To be honest, I noticed that you have a way with flowers. I noticed you'd made a beautiful arrangement from just two or three flowers and some leaves. You could do the same sort of thing for the house.'

Stephen's mother tipped her head to the side, and looked interested. 'Yes, I could, and I'd enjoy it, but what about the glasshouse? My hands won't allow me to do all the things necessary to grow flowers.'

'If Stephen buys suitable young plants from a good supplier, they only need protection from the wind, rain and cold, and someone to give them water and fertiliser. With hose connections in the right positions it would only mean you'd need to point the water at the pots. I'm sure you'd save Stephen a lot of money.'

Marjorie's eyes twinkled. 'Yes, I could manage that; especially if I keep my hands warm. If someone handles the potting, it should be quite easy.'

'I'm sure the supplier would position the pots when they deliver; and perhaps there's a village teenager who'd like to earn some pocket money helping you, if you find it's too much to manage the rest on your own.'

'It's a tempting idea! I must admit I'd love to do something constructive.'

Sara nodded. 'You'll have to try it

out, perhaps it will be too difficult for you, too painful, but it is worth a try. You like gardening . . . '

'And if I work in the glasshouse, I'm out of any wind and bad weather nearly all the time!'

'I can ask one of the men to fix an automatic system to open the fanlights for you on the hot days, electronics takes a little work out of gardening these days. I can even put an automatic watering system in, if watering by hand is too difficult for you.'

Marjorie nodded. 'It's a thought! But I'd like to try by hand first, if it is too painful, I can always get you back! And I'd save Stephen money in the long run, if I handle flower arrangements for the house, wouldn't I?'

'Bound to, although perhaps he's already thought about it, and made other plans.'

'Leave it to me! I'll talk to him about it.'

Marjorie looked at her watch. 'I came out to get parsley. I'm just about to have lunch, will you join me?'

Sara was tempted, she liked his mother, but she didn't want to intrude. 'Marjorie, you see enough of me all week!'

'Nonsense! It's nothing special — tomato soup with some fresh rolls. I just persuaded Stephen to join me.'

The temptation was too great. 'If you're sure I'm not intruding!'

Marjorie made a vague movement with her hand. 'Of course not. I'll just go and warm the rolls, and phone for Stephen to come down.'

Sara nodded. 'I'll take these things back to the car and change my shoes.'

A short time later Sara was seated in Marjorie's sitting room. She looked at a group of photos on the mantelpiece, and got up to take a closer look. Coming back from the kitchen with some cutlery, Marjorie stopped to explain who they were.

'That's my husband; the last time we were on holiday together, in Seville.'

Sara nodded. 'You both look very happy.'

'We were; it was in springtime and we just travelled from place to place as it took our fancy. There are some beautiful places in Spain. Have you ever been there?'

Sara shook her head. 'And that's Darren?'

Marjorie picked up the photo in question and studied it carefully. 'Yes.'

'He and Stephen look alike, don't they?'

'Yes. Lots of people say so.'

'Darren is not a common name either.'

She shrugged. 'My grandfather was called Darren. Names come and go, don't they?'

Sara smiled. 'Yes, my father is called Arthur, and I don't think many people would think of calling their baby Arthur these days!'

'Don't be so sure, if you look at the birth column in the newspaper, you'll find a lot of old-fashioned names.'

'His friends have always called him Art, probably because he didn't like being called Arthur.' She picked up a photo with Darren and Stephen standing side by side. 'What a pity!' Sara put the photo back gently.

'Yes, you keep asking why.' Marjorie put the photo she had in her hand back in place and picked up the cutlery again. 'Will you take these? I'll get on the house phone and tell Stephen the soup is ready.'

Stephen joined them a couple of minutes later. He nodded in her direction. 'Sara! A pleasant surprise! I didn't expect to see you today! Sherry? Mum?'

'Yes, please.'

His mother nodded, and he busied himself with the glasses. Handing Sara one of them, dark eyes met hazel for a fraction longer than necessary. He was wearing a fisherman's jersey with a white shirt peeping out from underneath, and faded jeans.

'What are you doing here today?'

She took a sip; the golden liquid covered her tongue and sharpened her taste. 'I'm catching up on paperwork. Your mother found me in the kitchen-garden, and took pity on me!'

He nodded, and with no special expression on his face he said. 'I know what it's like. Hard to refuse, isn't it? She thinks I'll fade away if she doesn't provide me with a hot meal sometimes!'

Marjorie was filling their dishes with soup. 'Rubbish! You manage very well, Stephen, I know that.'

Stephen sent Sara a wry expression across the table when his mother was passing a basket with hot crunchy rolls. She smiled back understandingly.

Sara broke her roll over her soup and golden crumbs sprinkled the surface to add more colour. The soup was freshly made. It was topped with a little fresh cream and sprinkled parsley. Stephen and Sara were both fervent in their praise.

Marjorie was pleased. 'A recipe from a magazine I was reading yesterday. I thought it sounded quite delicious, and it is.'

Sara felt Stephen's gaze embraced her more often than was strictly necessary, but a warning voice in her head told Sara not to ask why. The conversation rippled comfortably along.

Sara looked at her watch, and decided it was time to leave. She was surprised when Stephen suddenly asked.

'Would you like to see my part of the house? My flat?'

Sara was caught unawares.

Marjorie looked at them both for a moment. 'What a good idea! You've seen my part; Stephen can show you how these huge rooms can be turned into very modern living-quarters.'

The colour in Sara's cheeks had heightened. 'Yes, I'd like that. I'm curious!' She turned to his mother. 'But, I'll help with the washing-up first.'

Marjorie shook her head. 'Nothing for you to do! The saucepan and the dishes go in the dishwasher, but thanks for the offer.'

Sara watched Stephen as he rose in

one fluid movement and shoved his chair back in position. He walked towards the door, opened it, and stood demonstratively and hovering impatiently. They walked to the central staircase and went up the stairs to mid-level and then continued to the left. At the very top of the stairs, opening one of the doors leading off from the circular landing, Stephen moved ahead and she followed.

He lingered for a moment to give her a chance to catch up and turned slightly to talk to her as they walked down a short corridor painted white with touches of gilt; its long windows looked out over the lawns and formal garden. Sara figured they must be immediately above his mother's apartment.

His profile was sharp, but the sensitive mouth softened the firm features. He stopped in front of a solid cherry-coloured door and opened it, gesturing her to precede him.

They entered a huge sitting room. The white ceiling had been lowered, with rows of down-lights to provide lots of lighting. The original fireplace with its ornate white surround had been left intact, the wooden parquet floor glistened chestnut-gold in the sunshine from the windows opposite. The walls right and left of the fireplace were panelled in pale grey and the other walls had been painted plain white. Black and white dominated the room.

There were white bookcases full of brightly covered books from floor to ceiling along one wall, and a black leather couch and matching chairs were arranged around a glass coffee table near the fireplace.

She took a careful look around; her comment was spontaneous and honest. 'I like it very much. You've made yourself a very comfortable and spacious living room, it's hard to believe it was full of Georgian ornamentation before.'

'Yes. The original plasterwork is still there, above the present ceiling. Even though I still appreciate the beauty of it, I figure there's plenty left in the rest of the house. I wanted modern surroundings.'

Sara nodded understandingly and followed him through the other rooms. The dining room had a long oval table positioned directly beneath the room's original ornate oval ceiling. This had a dove coloured background with contrasting white plasterwork. The walls were painted an ivory tone.

The ten dining chairs surrounding the table were upholstered in matching tones. The afternoon sunshine caressed the honey coloured wooden floor, and wandered across the surface of the table to follow them as they continued into the adjoining kitchen.

The kitchen was ultra-modern in design, with lots of stainless steel, black granite working surfaces, and warm beech storage cupboards. The bar was part of the central working unit and it was lined with a couple of high stools.

There were two bathrooms. The first was en-suite to his bedroom and Sara had never seen a larger or more opulent one. It was marbled throughout and with lots of mirrors and a huge central bathtub.

At the end of the tour Sara's thoughts came back to earth. His flat illustrated the kind of wealth and the sort of world she'd only ever seen in glossy magazines before. She'd grown up in a semi-detached, where she'd had to fight her brother for possession of the bathroom every day to get to school on time.

She straightened her shoulders. She wasn't ashamed of her background; her mum and dad had given her the chance of a good education. Any burgeoning interest in Stephen began to fade with every new step in his kind of world.

They returned to the living room and he offered her something to drink. She accepted some mineral water and smiled up at him. 'Your flat is great; and it's hard for me to pick out any one single thing. I like everything. Did you have a professional interior designer, or is it all your own ideas?'

He gestured with one hand towards the couch for her to take a seat; his other hand was stuck in the pocket of his jeans. Sara was acutely conscious of his looks and his athletic physique. He poured himself a whisky from a cut-glass decanter, and sat down opposite. 'A mixture of both. I decided roughly what I needed, then a friend of mine, an interior designer, came down one weekend and made some suggestions.'

Sara took another sip, and then her mouth turned upwards as she gave him a ghost of a smile. 'Do you think you'll ever want to reverse things, turn the rooms back into their original appearance again?'

He shook his head slightly.

Sara liked the inherent strength in his face and the feeling he was a man who had things under control. His answer was not surprising; she knew how much Knowles House meant to him.

'I was just reluctant to destroy

plasterwork, or take out any of the wooden floors, etc. I suppose I didn't want to have the feeling I was the one who'd destroyed it forever. Basically it's still all there, if someone in the future ever wants to restore it.'

Sara emptied her glass. 'Thanks for the tour, Stephen. Your flat is beautiful. I'd better get back to my paperwork; it is the reason I stayed this weekend, instead of going home.'

He hesitated for a fraction. 'To someone special?'

She was surprised that he was interested, but he was probably only being polite. 'You mean a boyfriend? No . . . there was someone, until I came home to my flat one day a couple of months ago and found him with a stranger.'

His eyebrow lifted. 'The sort of situation you see in the cinema!'

She held his glance. 'It would have knocked me sideways anyway, but it was vile to come home and find them. He and I weren't even living together, I gave him a key because I was away so much and I was glad to know someone was keeping an eye on the flat. Once trust has been exploited that's it.'

'Do you wish you could turn back the clock?'

She didn't hesitate. 'You mean do I regret it? No! In a strange way I'm grateful that it happened now. I don't miss him, and realise it was an awful mistake, and wasn't love after all.'

'So you're not looking for a replacement?'

'No.'

'Has the fact that one man didn't know how well off he was, turned you into a confirmed career woman? Or will you get married, and have children one day?'

She noted the hidden compliment, coloured slightly, and shrugged. Her eyes froze on his long, lean form for a moment. 'I hope I'll be lucky enough to combine both, but I'll leave it up to fate. Marrying the wrong person for the wrong reason would be a huge disaster.'

She shrugged and looked at her watch. 'I'd better make a move, or I'll never finish my work. I've got a dog-eared brochure of places of interest and with luck I'm going to be a tourist tomorrow.' She put the glass down, gave him a smile and got up. 'There's a place called 'White Ladies' that sounds quite interesting. Do you know it?'

Hands in his pockets he said. 'Yes, it's about twenty miles away. I've heard of it, but never been there myself.'

She walked towards the door, and he followed. She half-turned towards him. 'I know my way out! Thanks for the tour!'

His answering smile was leisurely, his teeth strikingly white in a slightly tanned face. He followed her out to the circular landing. His voice drifted over her shoulder. 'I wouldn't mind seeing 'White Ladies' myself. We could go together tomorrow if you like, unless you'd rather go alone, of course.'

She stopped in her tracks and faced him again. She was so surprised she had no time to think rationally. 'No, of course not. I'd like that very much.'

'We could have a picnic, or is it the wrong time of year?'

'I don't think so; it's cool during the daytime, but not cold.'

'Fine, then I'll provide some chicken and a bottle of wine!'

'And I'll buy some other stuff, before I settle down to do some work again.'

He nodded. 'Good! I'll bring cutlery and glasses, etc. I've got a picnic-basket somewhere, and I'll pick you up about eleven?'

She looked at him and smiled. She didn't want to ask the questions bubbling in her brain, ones like, why he wanted to come, and how Lucy would react when she found out.

He lifted his hand in a gesture of farewell and vanished from sight.

6

It was a perfect day; white fluffy clouds high above, in a clear blue sky. She'd checked the weather forecast, and there was no mention of rain; so nothing could dampen her enthusiasm. She wished she had a proper picnic basket, but she made do with a backpack. Sara was ready by ten-thirty. Just before eleven, his car drew in opposite, and she grabbed her things.

He was coming for her but she beat him to it. He gave her a slow smile. 'You're on time again.' He opened the passenger door with a flourish. 'Give me that bag; I'll put it in the back.'

They were off. Sara was in high spirits and he was relaxed too. There was a lot of Sunday traffic on the roads but Stephen drove competently. She sunk into the leather seats and felt stress-free.

'White Ladies' was a moated manor house. The building was romantic to look at, the rooms inside were interesting to explore, and she was delighted to find the garden was laid out strictly to Tudor design. After a while Stephen left her to explore the gardens on her own and went to sit on a bench in the sun reading a Sunday newspaper he'd brought along. Sara meandered around the formally arranged grounds and took a closer look at the plants and the whole design. Eventually she came back to him.

Folding the paper he watched her approaching. 'Well? Was it good?'

'Umm! I've stored lots of information away in my brain, in case I'm ever confronted with a job that needs that sort of information. You can refer to books and pictures sometimes, and there is a lot of written information, but nothing is as good as seeing what it can look like in reality.'

He unfolded his long legs and got up. He looked young in fawn pants, a lightweight coffee coloured tweed jacket, and a white shirt — open at the neck. His face looked at ease.

'Ready for food? I haven't had anything since breakfast and I'm starving!'

Sara looked around and then nodded. 'It is lovely here, but I'm ready.'

He smiled and casually dropped his arm around her shoulder as they strolled in the direction of the exit. Sara noticed it, but pretended not to.

Back at the car he said, 'Ever heard of Rumsford Hill?'

'No.'

'It has some wonderful views of the surrounding countryside; I think the Royalists and Roundheads skirmished nearby, but I like it just because it's a great place to enjoy nature.'

'And it sounds like a perfect place to have a picnic!'

There were people walking the hill, and some had the same idea and were also having a picnic, but there was plenty of space. No-one was within distance of them when Stephen finally pulled into the side and they climbed a five-bar gate into the field next door. Sara admired the view down into the valley below.

She was delighted to just be with him. They seemed to complement each other and there was no tension. He liked her and she knew that, otherwise he would never have suggested the picnic.

She didn't intend to dwell on such thoughts for long, if she thought about Lucy (or perhaps other women) it would spoil everything. Stephen was young, he was attractive, and he had a special charisma that prevented the usual kind of rational deliberation. Today was hers.

'Have you got a rug by any chance?'

He gave her a knowing look. 'Put one in extra; one with a special backing so that we don't get wet from underneath however damp the ground is.'

He spread the large plaid on a patch of ground they'd cleared of bumpy twigs and stones. Sara began to unpack her bag and added her contributions to his. Soon he was stretched out on the rug with his arms tucked behind his head. He stared up at the sky; then his eyes stole a look in her direction. 'This is the life!'

Kneeling on the edge of the rug, her wide skirt spread around her, Stephen decided she was a very striking woman and an interesting companion to boot. He sat up and reached forward for a bottle of wine. He filled two long-stemmed glasses and handed her one. 'Here's to us!'

'To us! I'm glad you came and had the idea of having a picnic. I haven't been on a picnic for ages.'

'Neither have I! What have we got to eat? I've brought some chicken legs, cheese and some baguette.'

'Fresh?'

'Well, it is now. It was frozen until it saw the inside of my oven!'

'Perfect! I've got pâté, fruit juice, coffee and some cake.' She handed him a plate and a knife she'd borrowed from Elsie's kitchen.

'This reminds me of family picnics in France with Mum, Dad and Darren. We thought we were very cosmopolitan, picnicking in a foreign country.' He began to spread pâté on a chunk of bread. 'Glad you thought of coffee, I can't afford to have more than one glass of wine because of driving, but you can empty the bottle if you feel like it!'

She grinned. 'Trying to get me drunk?'

Leaning on one elbow he took a generous bite and replied, 'That's an interesting idea! Might be worth the effort! Tell me about your family.'

She did. How she grew up, about her parents, about her friends, about her hometown, and about her training. Time passed and the food diminished.

Sara sat with her arms locked around her knees. Stephen was sprawled on the other side of the rug most of the time and the remnants of their picnic lay between them.

A little while later he was drinking coffee; his long fingers encompassed the mug where steam was evaporating upwards in a faint white spiral. Sunlight spilled through the shifting leaves in the branches above their heads.

She asked, 'Do you miss London?'

'No, not really. It has lots of attractions, of course, all the entertainment and parties, the new people you meet all the time, that sort of thing, but I think I've adjusted to being back home and part of the local community again.'

'It sounds like you had a busy life!'

'I did, but everyone else lived at the same pace, so you took it for granted. I have a feeling it would have dulled with time. Life means more than money and parties, doesn't it?'

She couldn't imagine him as a partygoer and said so.

'There are parties, and parties. I don't like the ones with non-stop loud music and too much alcohol, but I enjoy quieter get-togethers or dinner parties where most of the people know each other quite well.'

Sara couldn't resist the temptation. 'Lots of girlfriends, I suppose?'

He shrugged. 'Not more than average, I suppose; but never met anyone who turned out to be special.'

'How long did you live there?'

'Seven . . . nearly eight years!'

'That's quite a long time!'

'Towards the end I wasn't in London most of the time, I was travelling a lot for the bank. That was great, because I could often arrange things so that I had a day or two's sightseeing when the business was completed. I don't suppose I would have seen as much of the world, if it hadn't been for that phase in my life.'

'Don't tell me where you've been, I'll turn green with envy!'

He laughed softly. 'Believe me, it wasn't all joy. All those long plane journeys, sudden changes in temperatures and climates, adjustments to different attitudes and different people all the time, but it was good to absorb the local atmosphere if I had a couple of hours free. You have to live somewhere for a while to say you know it, but you get a fleeting impression even if you only have half a day, or a weekend to explore.'

'Which place did you enjoy most?'

'Umm! Hard to say! Hong Kong perhaps, or Singapore, or Australia.'

She looked at him quietly. 'Coming back to run the estate must have been a complete contrast to your previous lifestyle. Do you regret having done so?'

He shook his head firmly. 'I had to get used to it, and I don't just mean the work. I'd forgotten how quiet and tranquil it is around the place. I don't regret it now, not a bit. I'm sure my father and brother would have wanted me to take over, and that is the silent encouragement that makes me do the best I can.'

It was only because the sun was low and sending shadows up the slope that they both remembered that life awaited them below.

He looked at her with her arms wrapped around herself. 'It's getting a bit chilly, isn't it? I suppose we should make a move?'

She nodded reluctantly, and looked at her watch. 'It'll be getting dark soon.' Sara started to gather the remains together. 'Take the rest of the pâté, I can't keep it, and it's a pity to throw it away.' She added it to his basket. She pushed the plates and rest of the rubbish into an extra plastic bag and stuffed everything into her backpack.

Stephen stood his basket to one side, and they both bent down to pick up the plaid. They were inches apart; she held her breath as he moved towards her and she knew he was going to kiss her. Pleasure unfolded inside her and her body came alive when he did. Sara had never felt that a mere kiss could bring so much pleasure before. His dark brown eyes stared searchingly at her face and his breathing was uneven. She could see the fine lines at the edge of his eyes; she was a little confused by the situation.

'Thank you for a really nice day, Sara Maxwell!'

All her senses were still tingling but she tried to be nonchalant. 'I'm the one who should say 'thank you', you shared today with me. It was lovely!' She smiled and wished with all her heart that he'd kiss her again. He didn't. She mused that he had probably kissed dozens of women before in similar situations — the kiss meant nothing special.

He got up, surprisingly elegantly for someone who was so tall, and offered her his hand. She took it, and found just the feeling of his fingers had the power to stir her now. He let her hand fall and bent down, to retrieve and fold the plaid. He collected the rest of the things, including her rucksack and deposited them in the car waiting on the other side of the fence.

The journey back was uneventful and they spent it mostly in companionable silence. He pointed out some places of interest on the way; he clearly knew the surrounding countryside very well. There was music playing on the radio, and the sunshine, low on the horizon. It spilled through the car windows in broken splashes as it outfoxed the hedges and buildings as they sped past.

Sara wondered if he'd suggest a farewell drink in the pub, but when they reached the 'Smith's Arms', he didn't. He retrieved her backpack and handed it to her when she got out. There were people milling about in front of the pub door, and he raised his hand in greeting to some people in the crowd. 'See you tomorrow?'

Sara smiled. 'I expect so. Thanks again, Stephen. I enjoyed myself very much.'

He gave her an answering smile. 'So did I.'

Not wanting to make him wait, people were eyeing them with undue interest, she walked away. He got into the BMW again, reversed out of the parking lot, and nodded briefly in her direction before he picked up speed and faded from sight at the end of the village. She went inside, climbed the stairs and closed the door to her bedroom. She leaned against it and wrapped her arms around herself. It had been a perfect day.

Next day, Sara was disappointed that she only saw him from waving distance. He made no special effort to join her but she knew from a passing conversation with Alan that he had visitors who wanted to buy some breeding cattle.

She got on with her work. That evening Alan roped her in to play darts with some of the regulars. She and Alan were wedged between the others at one of the small round tables in the bar, waiting for their turn, and talking. Sara's wanderings came to a sudden end when she realised he was asking her to be his partner at a local dance.

She was pleased because it showed her that other men were anxious for her company even if Stephen wasn't. It would be futile to sulk in the corner, in the hope that Stephen would pay her the sort of attention she longed for. She needed a distraction and Alan was a nice person. 'When is it?'

'Next Saturday!'

'That's fine, yes I'd like to come. Is it a formal affair?'

Alan smiled broadly and shrugged. 'The men have to wear dark suits.'

Some slight furrows buried themselves in her forehead briefly and she tilted her head. 'And what do the women wear?'

He looked a little helpless. 'I don't know; dresses I suppose!'

'Alan, that is the least helpful description of clothing I've ever heard! You are hopeless!'

He shrugged. 'I've never taken much notice.'

Sara's eyes twinkled and she laughed softly. 'You recognise a cow from five hundred yards away, but you don't remember what women wear to a dance?'

'I don't pay any attention to that sort of thing. You'd better ask someone else, a woman.'

She decided on a rust coloured silk taffeta cocktail dress she'd worn at the evening celebrations of a cousin's wedding a couple of months ago. It was strapless with a full knee length bubble skirt, had a fitted bodice and a decorative bow with sequined details at waist level. She arranged her hair behind her ears, took special care with her make-up, added a pair of sparkling long earrings and completed the outfit with a silver evening bag and matching sandals.

'Wow!' Alan made a complimentary bow and then hurried to help her don her coat. 'No-one would believe this vision before me is the same woman who spends most of her time up to her knees in muck all day. A real-day Cinderella-like transformation. I hope you don't change, and look like you've climbed out of a pigsty again at the stroke of midnight.'

112

Sara took an imaginary swipe at him with her bag and smiled. 'I take it there's a hidden compliment in there somewhere?' She eyed him in his dark suit and conservative tie. 'I must say you don't look bad either!'

He grinned and offered her his arm. 'Shall we . . . ?'

The Young Farmers' Annual Dance was held in the ballroom of a large hotel in the next market town. Places at the tables had been organised according to the ticket numbers. Sara and Alan found their table easily; Alan knew some of the others; Sara didn't. Everyone was friendly and wanted to enjoy themselves; that was all that mattered.

A tasty hot evening meal was part of the festivities; and then annual awards were presented to their winners for special achievements within the farming community. Before a lot of the guests began to get too restless, and too many men began to think about escaping to the bar for a drink, the floor was at last cleared for dancing.

Sara had always enjoyed dancing. Alan tried his best but didn't always succeed. For his part, Alan felt really pleased she'd agreed to come this evening, and apart from his lack of dancing skills, it was going well. Alan wished he'd taken the time to learn more than how to sway from one foot to the other. He liked Sara and speculated on whether he could interest her in more than friendship.

There was a live band playing ballroom dances, party dances, and splashes of disco music for the younger generation. After a couple of rounds Alan went off to get her something to drink and she stood in the shadows on the side, midst a lot of people gathered in groups talking, or like her, watching the crowded dance-floor.

'Hello, Sara!'

His voice sent a shiver of surprise down her spine. She looked up and saw Stephen, with Lucy at his side. Lucy's eyes narrowed as she viewed Sara; it was a look of critical assessment. Stephen's look was admiring and full of approval.

'H . . . hello! Stephen, Lucy!'

'Good heavens, Sara! I didn't expect to see you here tonight.' Lucy wore a full-length black chiffon gown with a halter neckline and a criss-cross back. The bodice had been worked with a dainty beaded floral pattern. Her make-up was perfect, and her hair styled in a firm chignon.

Somehow Lucy reminded Sara of pictures of Grace Kelly. Lucy had deliberately cultivated her aura of sophistication and refinement and somehow Sara guessed that Lucy didn't feel at ease among some of the people present. Most of them were too down to earth for Lucy's tastes, too tied to the land, and they called a spade a spade.

At least Sara knew she looked as good as Lucy for once tonight, perhaps even better. Sara decided an explanation of her presence was called-for. 'Alan invited me. I didn't think you'd be here either. Although of course it's more logical for you to be here than me, isn't it?' Was it just her fancy, or did Sara see a flicker cross Stephen's face at Alan's name.

Lucy's voice clarified her position and explained Stephen's involvement. 'I help to organise it, and Stephen is chairman of one of the local Farmer's Association.'

Sara looked at them both and said. 'Oh, I see!' She was grateful when Alan returned. Once greetings had been exchanged between them all, he handed Sara her glass and she took a grateful sip. The band began to play a new series of tunes.

'Like to dance, Sara?'

She was taken aback, looked at Stephen for a moment, but nodded. He took her glass, handed it to Alan and held out his hand. 'You'll give Lucy the benefit of your company, won't you, Alan?'

Alan looked uneasy at the idea, but only Sara noticed it. Lucy was too busy watching Stephen. Her eyes were hooded, and Sara had the feeling Lucy was not happy with the way the evening was going.

Sara put her hand in Stephen's outstretched one, and they joined the others on the dance-floor. Somehow Sara knew he'd dance well. She felt she was dancing on air with him holding her close. She leaned toward him, her face inches away from his shoulder.

His dark eyebrow arched mischievously, he looked down. 'You look sensational! I haven't seen you for a while. I've been busy with buyers, and away for a couple of days.'

She coloured at the compliment, noted his explanation, but was lost for words. She concentrated on following his lead and searched for something neutral to talk about. In his dinner jacket he was more attractive than ever, and she loved the feeling of being with him.

Her breath seemed constricted and she had to make a desperate attempt to resist his smile. She'd danced with lots of other men, but no one else had ever had an effect like this before. She had to remind herself firmly that Stephen was Lucy's partner.

He commented. 'You dance properly. Most people only want to shuffle around the floor these days.'

Sara pulled herself together and tried to ignore the feeling the hand on her bare back, was causing inside her. The other hand held her hand firmly, and their bodies touched. 'My parents love ballroom dancing, and they decided I ought to be able to follow my partner correctly so I had to have lessons.'

She gave in to the sensation of being with him. He smelt of soap and leather, and a unique smell of his own; warm and slightly lemony. It was pointless to pretend she didn't care, the longer she knew him the stronger she felt about him. They danced on, and he captured her eyes with his for a moment; they seemed to be reaching into her thoughts.

The sound of music carried them along, and Sara wished the tune would never end, but it did, and people began to escort their partners back to their tables. Still on the dance-floor, their hands loosened and they parted. He studied her thoughtfully for a moment before he placed a hand in the small of her back and they walked back through the remaining dancers to where Alan was waiting with a visibly impatient Lucy.

The rest of the evening went well. Sara knew it wasn't fair on Alan, but it was hard for her not to search for Stephen in the crowded room all the time. She tried to pull herself together and made an effort to concentrate on her partner. Now and then Sara did glimpse Lucy and Stephen. She caught his eye and smiled in their direction. His expression was good-humoured and once he lifted his glass. Sara surmised that Lucy would take care that he fulfilled his responsibilities as a committee member and that he wouldn't have any more spare time for her tonight.

Alan dropped her off at the pub in the early hours of the morning.

She leaned across and gave him a brief kiss on the cheek. 'Thank you for a lovely evening Alan. I enjoyed it.'

In the darkness his eyes twinkled in the dark. 'I did too. Perhaps we can do something together again soon, although not necessarily dancing!'

She laughed gently. 'Oh, you're not that bad. You get round the floor quite competently. You might turn out to be a second Fred Astaire with a little practice!'

'If you'll be my Ginger Rogers, I might think seriously about that!'

Sara didn't answer. She didn't want to waken any false hopes. Alan didn't deserve that.

Getting ready for bed she stared into the mirror in the bathroom and admitted with a sense of inner release that she'd fallen in love with Stephen Dumont. She'd never be happy with second-best.

7

On Monday morning, disconcerted by the effect of seeing him coming in her direction, she looked pointedly away. She experienced a gamut of perplexing emotions and hadn't yet figured out how to retain control of her feelings. Just the sight of him overwhelmed her. Reminding herself that Stephen had always been friendly and polite to her, but apart from that one kiss when they shared a picnic he'd never indicated more than friendship. It helped her to remain cool.

There was also the undeniable fact that Lucy was always in the background. Sara would disappear from his life in a few weeks time; if she concentrated on that fact, it might help her to get through.

Sara found she couldn't just pretend to be buried in her work; he was coming purposely in her direction. It was hard to remain coherent when her pulse was out of control and she had collywobbles in her stomach. She drew a deep breath, looked up and parted her lips in a welcoming smile.

He seemed in an exuberant mood. Their eyes met and she felt a shock run through her. She forced herself to greet him naturally. 'Morning! Isn't it wonderful weather? I thought I'd concentrate on finishing off the sunken garden this morning. The men have already planted the boxwood and laurels, I'm filling in the gaps.' She gestured towards an assortment of pots on a wooden tray filled with other plants.

She mused for the umpteenth time that his eyes were a very dark brown, almost black, and they held her attention completely for a few seconds when his glance wandered over her face. His interest moved on to what she was doing. 'That looks good. My mother's enthusiasm grows and grows, especially because the long-range view from the house hasn't changed at all!'

'That's why this type of garden is so brilliant, it provides a pretty focal point right next to the house while not spoiling any long-distant view of the surrounding garden and countryside. It's the same principal as a ha-ha.'

He stared at her baffled. 'A what?'

Bantering with him helped to relax her manner, she said. 'A ha-ha, it was a sort of deep dry ditch with steep banks, or sometimes a freestanding wall within a ditch, below site level. It replaced a park wall or a fence, and prevented animals or unwanted visitors straying into the garden. The ha-ha made the surrounding countryside part of the garden, and was a practical solution for fixing the boundaries around the house.'

With dry amusement in his voice he replied: 'You learn something everyday!'

He chuckled. 'I can understand why previous generations might have wanted privacy. The only negative thought I have about throwing open the house to the public so far is the fact that strange people will be wandering around the garden, but you can't make an omelette without breaking eggs, if we offer the house for holding events, we have to take that sort of thing in our stride.'

She nodded. 'And you won't have bookings every day of every week; most of the time there'll be no-one else around. The house will be yours again. When you know there's a celebration going on, you'll just have to get used to avoiding certain places on that day. Luckily your mother is a very sociable person, so if she bumped into strangers I don't think she'll mind too much.' She looked up and said playfully: 'Keep thinking about the money; that will always help.'

He threw back his head and laughed then he considered her for a moment and then he offered her a sudden, arresting smile again before he said, 'I just hope it works out.'

'Oh, I'm sure it will! There is no place locally that offers the kind of space and atmosphere you have here. I can imagine all the brides-to-be within a radius of fifty miles will be falling over themselves to book it. Once you've gained a reputation, other things like silver weddings, confer-ences, family get-togethers will come automatically.' She played with the trowel in her hand. 'Have you thought about offering it as a site for television or film productions?'

He looked startled for a moment, but then pleased. 'Do you know something, I hadn't! It's another possibility worth thinking about.'

They shared a smile.

'Why don't you find out? There's bound to be lots of information on the Internet; you can get an insight on what's involved.'

He stuck his hands into the pockets of his weatherproof jacket. The breeze ruffled his hair and he nodded back without speaking for a moment. After a slight pause he said. 'Enjoy yourself on Saturday?'

'Yes!'

'Good!' He gave her a grudging nod. 'If Lucy had known you were coming, I'm sure she'd have put us all on the same table.'

Sara doubted it, but she didn't comment.

'My mother told me about your idea of putting her in charge of flower arrangements in the house, and overseeing the glasshouse.'

Sara saw a beginning of a smile that tipped the corner of his mouth; she was relieved that he seemed to approve. Sara felt a little flustered; she took a moment to catch her breath. 'Was it wrong of me to suggest it?'

'No, in fact it is a very good idea; it will give her something to do again. I think she'd enjoy it very much. She mentioned that you told her not to tell me it was your brainchild — why?'

Her heart thumped erratically. 'I thought you'd be sceptical if she did.'

'Why should I be? I admit I don't grab innovations suggested by someone else, but I don't doubt your motives any more. It certainly isn't part of your job to help employers save money. If my mother handled that side of the flowers it would.'

Sara flushed a bright pink. 'I'm not always right, but I honestly think it would be good for your mother and the house. She says she used to enjoy gardening, so caring for the flowers in the glasshouse, and doing the flower arrangements in the house, would be an ideal occupation.'

'I agree! If she doesn't keep a certain degree of mobility, the joints may stiffen up even faster. She'd love a task of her own.' He opened his mouth to say something else, but they were interrupted by the appearance of one of the workers, hurrying towards Sara.

He nodded to Stephen and took his chance to explain. 'Sara! Harry doesn't know where to plant the rest of the boxwood plants! He's waiting for you over by the far fence.'

Standing behind him Stephen looked at her and shrugged silently. 'No peace for the wicked, I see!' He lifted his hand in farewell and strode off in the direction of the house.

Marjorie Dumont beckoned to her. Sara had a wooden tray with pots of winter flowering pansies in her arms. Sara put them down on the steps, took off her gloves, and went briskly across the terrace to where she was standing at the open French window.

'Stephen thought the idea of me and the flower arrangements was good.' She sounded happy and pleased.

Sara smiled briefly. 'I know; he told me so too.'

'He talked to you about it? Oh! . . . ' She looked a bit self-conscious. ' . . . I hope you don't mind, I didn't intend to mention it was your idea; it sort of slipped out.'

Sara smiled reassuringly. 'Even if he'd been against it, I'm used to coping with the fact that people don't always agree with my suggestions. Stephen is very fair, in comparison to a lot of other employers I've had. I didn't want to push you into doing something that was wrong for you, because of your rheumatism!'

There was a spark of gaiety in her voice. 'I'm not stupid Sara, I'll protect my hands as much as I can. No-one knows better than I do that if I don't take care, my hands will play up.'

'I certainly don't think that you're stupid.' Sara looked across the open countryside. 'Isn't it lovely today? These early autumn days are so beautiful!' She took a deep breath. 'Even the earth has a special smell to it'

Mrs Dumont nodded. 'Do you work outside in the winter too?'

Sara's expressive face was full of good humour. 'Yes! I can't pretend that I like it, but sometimes it can't be avoided. Some of the jobs we get are very comprehensive, and so complex, that we have to. You can still build walls, pathways, lay drainage, or do other kinds of preparation work even if it's really cold, but usually planting comes to a halt in winter.

'Most of us use up the overtime we put in at other times of the year to go on holiday. My boss, Brian, likes that. He can calculate his costs better, and he doesn't have to put good people off in the winter and search for help again when he needs it the following year. Personally, I spend a lot time in the office in winter, making plans, organising the kind of supplies we always need, and getting them stored properly. We also use the time to overhaul and clean all the machinery. We are busy, but the pressure is off.' Her voice heightened. 'I go on holiday in winter, where it's warm and sunny!'

'I bet!' Marjorie liked Sara more and more. She was someone who didn't complain, got on with her job, and made the best out of her life. 'What about a coffee?'

'Thanks, but I must get on. We have to get the smaller plants in, and a couple of big trees are due to arrive this afternoon. We have to get things planted straight away so that they'll acclimatise before the really cold weather starts.'

'How much longer will you be here, Sara?'

'A couple of weeks at the most.'

Marjorie looked at her thoughtfully. 'You've made a big difference to the place, and I'm not just talking about the sunken garden. A lot of people might not notice, but I do. I've lived here most of my life.'

'Next spring you'll see it — when the bushes bloom, and the new trees show contrasting spots in the landscape!'

'We must keep in touch!'

Sara didn't think that was a good idea. She didn't want to be troubled by hearing about Stephen and Lucy's engagement, or their marriage, or about how Lucy was fitting into her new role. Sara nodded without commenting and tried to look pleased. 'I must get on!'

Marjorie nodded understandingly.

When Stephen married and Lucy moved into his flat upstairs, there'd be a lot more life in the house to divert her, and in a couple of years there might be grandchildren running around the gardens. The though of Lucy having Stephen's child was like a sharp knife cutting at her insides. She turned away swiftly and hurried back to pick up the tray of flowers on the steps.

8

It was Friday afternoon and for once Sara was almost glad to be going home. She'd avoided working near the house for some days, so that she wouldn't accidentally bump into Stephen. She was trying to ease herself out of a situation that was bound to make her feel miserable. If she tried to lessen the effect of leaving him now, it would be the first step of accepting reality and getting on with her life as best she could.

All of her workers had left hours ago; they were always anxious to get away punctually on a Friday. She'd also spotted Stephen's car speeding down the drive a short time ago. When she reached her car, she changed out of her wellingtons, took off her padded jacket and put them in the boot with the rest of her things. At last she was ready to leave but then her car wouldn't start.

'Blast!' She got out and poked around in the engine, without really knowing what she was doing. Diffused light was fighting its way through the low white clouds, it wasn't real sunshine, just mellow autumn light.

The accompanying breezes were cool. Darker clouds were gathering in the west, and it wouldn't be long until it started to rain. She sighed. It was no use; she'd have to find help. Her best chance was the estate office; perhaps Alan was still there, if not she'd have to get the telephone number of a local garage from Marjorie. She put her jacket back on.

At the office she cupped her hands round her eyes and peered through the windowpane. It was dark and quiet everywhere, and there was no sign of anyone. Sara now hoped that Marjorie wasn't out on one of her rare trips to the village; if she wasn't at home, Sara would have to walk to the village to get help.

She stuck her hands in her pockets and began to walk towards the house. As she turned the corner, she almost ran straight into Stephen. She coloured, felt vulnerable because of her whirling emotions, and had the feeling he was studying her with curious intensity.

'I thought you must still be here; I noticed your car parked out front.'

Looking up at him, her emotions split in two directions. She was anxious to escape from the effect of his presence, but she couldn't ignore the warm flow of happiness he gave her, just being so close. 'Something's wrong with my car. I was hoping to find Alan in the office, but he's gone already. I was going to try your mother, to see if I could telephone the village for help.'

His lips narrowed. 'Alan hasn't been here all day. He's out at an auction the other side of Newbury. My mother is visiting a friend in hospital. Perhaps I can help?'

She accepted his offer without words and started to walk towards the front of the house. He fell into step beside her.

He said casually, 'I haven't seen much of you lately.'

Sara was happy he'd noticed she hadn't been around, but she didn't allow herself the luxury of placing too much importance on his words. 'I've been working along the boundaries.'

He nodded. 'What's wrong with the car?'

She shrugged. 'I haven't the slightest idea! It wouldn't start.'

Minutes later he let the lid of the bonnet fall with a loud thud. 'From the sound of it I think it may be the ignition, but I'm not much of a mechanic. The best thing is to get Bill from the garage to take a look.'

Sara took a look at her watch. 'Blast! I was on my way home. It's important this weekend.'

He viewed her expression with a blank look. 'You still can. If you leave the car here, I'll sort it out with Bill. There's a train leaving in roughly an hour that will take you home, you come from near Bristol, don't you? I know the times of trains going in that direction because I looked it up for a visitor recently. Someone can meet you there, or perhaps there's a bus home from the station?'

'My dad would come for me!'

'Then it's settled. I'll drive you to the pub, and you can collect your case and phone your parents from there. I'll call at the garage; ask Bill to sort out the car trouble.'

He didn't wait for her reply, and started to walk towards his car. It was just as well, her mind was in a turmoil trying to deal with all the emotions, which his voice and his sheer presence wakened in her.

She got in and fixed the safety belt. Feeling disconcerted, she looked ahead out of the windscreen and tried to calm her thoughts as he drove down the tree-lined driveway. A few minutes in Stephen's company were enough to completely break down her resistance and destroy her resolution not to crave after him. He fired her imagination and wakened longings in a way no other man had ever done before.

An hour later, with her in the passenger seat, he pulled up in front of the station. They got out and he took her suitcase from the boot. Placing his free hand under her elbow, he guided her through the old-fashioned station entrance. Sara didn't resist; he gave her a feeling of safety and security.

On the windy platform they joined a couple of others who were also waiting for the train. 'We're in plenty of time.' He deposited her case on the ground, and looked briefly in the direction the train was due to come. 'If you phone and let me know the arrival time, I'll pick you up when you come back.'

She opened her mouth to protest, but he forestalled by lifting his hand. 'It's no problem. It takes me ten minutes to get here from the house, I'm home all day Sunday. I'll put you in the picture about your car then.'

What was the point in arguing? She nodded hastily. 'If you're sure it's no trouble. Thanks for the offer.' She pulled some stray strands of hair out of her face with her fingers.

He asked casually, 'Something special happening on the weekend, I gather?'

There was a flush on her pale cheeks. 'My parents are celebrating their 30th wedding anniversary, and my brother, his wife, and I are taking them out for a meal and a visit to the theatre. It's important for me to be there, otherwise I wouldn't leave you to sort out my problems like this.'

She looked at him and stored away the picture of his attractive dark figure in a Barbour jacket, dark blue sweater and matching blue chinos.

His lips parted in a display of straight white teeth. 'Don't give it another thought.' The sound of the approaching train silenced them both, and once it drew to a halt, she got in. Doors were slamming along its length. He handed her the suitcase and his hand lingered a moment too long as their fingers touched.

Sara swallowed hard and squared her shoulders. 'Thanks, Stephen!'

'Don't mention it!' He eyed her closely before he closed the door and stepped back; the train was about to leave. He stood waiting for the train to pull out. When it did, his eyes followed its snaking form until it disappeared from his sight. He was a silent, solitary figure on the empty station platform.

Unknown to him, at the same time, Sara was flattening her nose against the window in an attempt to look aslant through the window and keep him in sight.

* * *

Stephen was waiting on the grimy platform, and his welcoming smile was genuine. 'Well, what was it like? How did the weekend go?'

Sara felt a warm glow, blissfully happy and fully alive. 'I think my parents were taken completely by surprise! My mother had planned a special meal for us, but they didn't reckon we'd turn the tables on them. They're not the kind of people who like a lot of fuss, but I'm sure they were delighted with the way the whole evening went. To crown it all, my brother and his wife announced they're expecting a baby — I'm going to be an auntie!'

He looked at her excited expression and amusement flickered in his eyes. 'The icing on the top of the cake, I expect?'

'Definitely.' Walking at his side the two of them reached his car. 'I won't be surprised to hear my mother is on a shopping spree for baby clothes tomorrow morning! Darren and Helen have been married for six years and I think they've been hoping for a baby for some time now.'

Stephen deposited her case, and opened the passenger door.

She got in, and started to think about

more mundane problems. 'What about my car?'

'It was the ignition.'

She was still absorbing the pleasure of seeing him waiting for her on the platform. 'What about the bill?'

'I told him to drop it off at the pub.' He was fixing his safety belt. 'He mentioned something, roughly £110 I think.'

'Botheration! But there's no point in complaining; I need a car. I haven't really had any trouble with it before. I wonder why the ignition suddenly gave up the ghost? Where is it now?'

'The garage picked it up from the house, and they brought it back there. Bill didn't understand me when I told him he could leave it at the pub. You'd better come with me and pick it up now otherwise you'll have to walk from the village tomorrow morning.'

Sara nodded and looked out of the window as they sped along. Although the weather didn't encourage much outside activities, there were a couple of hardly recognisable figures battling the wind on the pavement of the village street. He waved to someone she didn't know.

'Everyone knows you, don't they?'

'I suppose so. The local community is still fairly intact, and although a lot of new faces have moved into the village, the pace of things hasn't altered much.'

'Wasn't it a bit of a drag? Did people expect you and your brother to behave in a certain way all the time, because you came from the 'big' house?'

The warmth of his smile echoed in his voice. 'Oh, it wasn't like that. My parents never instilled any kind of snobbishness in us; in fact they did the opposite. They tried to make us understand we would only become what we wanted to be through our own efforts. It was up to us, life didn't owe us anything. There was always the feeling of being responsible for the house and the land, but not in a 'holier-than-thou' way.

'We went to the local primary school,

the local grammar school, went to boy scouts meetings, attended the church, and got up to the usual kind of mischief other boys in the village did. If people handled us differently, it wasn't because my parents wanted it. If we got into trouble people told my father and he dealt with it like any other father.'

'Did you get into trouble? What did you do?'

'Oh, the usual kind of pranks! Leaving the gate open for the bull to get out, knocking doors and running off, playing Robin Hood up in the woods and frightening passers-by out of their wits, that sort of thing. Nothing serious!'

Sara laughed. 'I can't say that I'd like to suddenly meet a bull in the wrong place!'

He shrugged and looked across briefly, merriment in his eyes. 'Neither did our teacher from the village. She made a hell of a fuss, and we had to make amends for a whole month in her garden. I genuinely enjoy sharing a pint with people from the village, they are part of my life and I like most of them!'

By now they'd driven past the evenly spaced row of trees leading up to Knowles House and he came to a stop next to her car. Sara unfastened her belt and got out.

'Thanks, Stephen!'

He slammed the car door and retrieved her case. 'My mother wants you to come in for a coffee, if you have time.' He took her keys out of his pocket, put the case in the boot, locked it, and then handed them to her.

Against the background of the boughs of the trees with their shifting leaves, he looked tall and powerful. She played with the keys. 'I ought to be getting back to the pub.'

He tucked his hand under her elbow. 'Oh, come on! She'll be disappointed if you rush off.'

She threw caution to the wind and went.

It felt a bit like coming home. No restraint, no uneasiness. She was with people she liked, who seemed to like her. Stephen stayed, and she told his mother about the weekend again. Stephen listened a second time without any apparent sign of boredom.

'How lovely; and what good news to top it all! I bet your mother is excited?'

'It's early days yet, but yes, she's over the moon. She loves children.'

'So do I, but we're so far from the village, I've never had the chance to be with other people's children for long, and I've become a strange and distant figure for most of the small children now.'

Sara gathered her courage and looked at him. 'Stephen can change that situation for you. Perhaps you'll have a new generation of Dumonts populating the grounds again one day!'

He lifted his eyebrows. His eyes were intent and appraising but there were laughter lines around his mouth. He didn't comment.

'Do you like children, Sara?'

'Yes! I haven't actually given much

thought to the idea, but yes, I do like children.'

Marjorie nodded in approval. 'Oh, I tried the watering system in the glasshouse yesterday. It works well. I didn't have it on for long, I didn't want to freeze up the system when the cold weather starts.'

Sara sipped her coffee and listened to Stephen and his mother talking about the catering firms who were interested in handling the receptions and celebrations. She knew there was a huge kitchen in the basement; with double sinks and cupboards that were full of crockery and glass.

There was also a twelve-hob oven, and yards of working space. Apparently several companies were already enthusiastically making presentations and plans in competition with each other.

The sun had gone. Sara got up. 'Thanks for the coffee, Marjorie. I'll be off.'

'See you tomorrow, I hope?'

Sara nodded. 'Perhaps. Almost my

last week!' She went out through the French windows. The wind was cool and blowing gently from the direction of the open pastures. She looked at the purple shadows in the folds and hollows of the hills. Despite her protest, Stephen came with her to her car.

She opened the car door and looked up at him. She opened her mouth to say something, but to her overwhelming surprise he leaned forward and kissed her gently like a whisper; it sent shock waves through her entire body. Her heart hammered against her ribs and their eyes locked as their breathing came in unison.

It left her wanting more, and confirmed what she already believed, Stephen was the man she wanted. No-one else would ever do. The wind ruffled her hair and she felt her knees weaken. His eyes flickered in the fading light. Neither of them spoke for a moment and Sara had the feeling that he was just as startled and confused about the situation as she was.

Stephen opened his mouth to say something, but the screech of brakes as Lucy brought her car to a halt interrupted him. Lucy got out with unaccustomed haste and walked purposely towards them. Sara guessed she had seen them kissing as she came up the drive.

She didn't want to face Lucy now; that would spoil the moment. Whether his kiss was a mistake or a meaningless whim of the moment, didn't make any difference to Sara, she wanted to savour the memory. She got into her car and started the engine. Her colour was high, but no-one would notice. She raised her hand in the direction of Stephen as she reversed and drove off down the avenue of trees on the way back to the village.

Her thoughts were a maelstrom. She parked her car, and took her case upstairs to her room. She was much too agitated to do anything, so she grabbed a jacket and went out again. She walked through the village, as far as the petrol station at the other end. The remaining daylight was enough to encourage her to leave the main road and cut down a nearby lane.

She barely noticed how the soaking grass alongside the road was saturating her trousers. She stopped at a five bar gate to stare at a group of horses who were still poking around under the trees. Their stable door was open, but they were clearly reluctant to go in for the night. Listening to their whinnying, her thoughts circled and her heart questioned why Stephen had kissed her? Was it just an impetuous action of his, or an intentional one?

Lucy had always made it clear that she had unconfirmed rights to Stephen, that their relationship was all a foregone conclusion. If that was true, Stephen wasn't acting fair. Sara found that was hard to believe — he wasn't that kind of man. Perhaps he'd just felt kindly towards her, and expressed it by kissing her.

Her eyes were misted. She shoved her

hands back into the pockets of her jacket, and set out for the pub again. Somewhere in the distance a dog was barking, and there was a smell of fish and chips as she passed the small shop on the silent main street.

If she kept her mind on her work she might be able to leave the district without too many scars on her soul. She loved him of course she did; he was all she'd ever wanted, but there were more things pushing them apart, than bringing them together.

9

Sara went to the estate office, her heart beating fast, and a small knot in her stomach. She knocked and went in. A quick glance told her Stephen wasn't there. 'I was looking for Stephen.'

'Just went out; five minutes ago.' Alan noticed the tense expression on her face, and wondered what was wrong. Sara was usually a very relaxed character. 'I think he went off towards the house, but I'm not sure. Anything I can do?'

She found her voice with difficulty and gave him a weak smile. 'No — no, nothing important. I just wanted to give him these.' She lifted a sheaf of papers. 'I'll just see if he's in the house.'

Alan nodded, and she left. He watched her through the window as she crossed the yard, and wondered why Stephen didn't appreciate how lucky he was.

Sara looked around on the way. There was no sign of him. He must have gone out, or into the house. She sighed, torn between wanting to see him, and wanting to avoid him. She set out to circle the house, and head back to the estate office. It was a beautiful late September morning.

She met Marjorie, dressed and on her way to the garage. She smiled at Sara. 'I'm off to town. I've a shopping list of things I've run out of, and I have to go to the doctors for a new prescription.'

'Well, you've chosen a lovely day.'

Marjorie nodded. 'I'll treat myself to lunch, change my library books and meet a friend of mine for coffee.'

'A full programme! I was looking for Stephen to give him these lists of the things we've planted, so that he can check them when the bill comes in.'

'I haven't seen him this morning, but I have a feeling that I saw his car going down the drive not so long ago. Why don't you just put them on his desk in the library? He's sure to find them there; he goes there to work if he wants some peace and quiet. People are in and out of the estate office all the time.' She turned. 'I'll unlock the front door, and you can pull it behind you when you leave.'

The prospect of avoiding him face to face was tempting. So Sara nodded.

Her team of workers were busy around the house for the last time; completing the last touches and tidying the garden before they gathered their tools together for the last time. Sara was storing pictures in her mind, and making others with her digital camera; she wouldn't be coming back.

Normally she always enjoyed seeing how her ideas came to life, and she often went back to former workplaces to check on progress and talk to the owners. This time was different. She hadn't seen Stephen since Sunday evening. Was it coincidence or intention? She'd gone out of her way to avoid the house, and she'd no professional reason to consult him anymore. He hadn't sought her company. Perhaps he was embarrassed and evading her too.

On Wednesday afternoon, as she was walking across the lawn towards the potting shed, she was surprised to see Lucy frantically beckoning her from the main entrance. She went towards her and waited for an explanation when she reached the foot of the steps.

'Can you come in, Sara?' Lucy didn't wait for an answer, turned and went inside.

Puzzled Sara went after her, removing her muddy shoes beforehand, and leaving them outside. Marjorie stood in the doorway to her rooms, and Stephen stood at the foot of the stairs; his eyebrows lifted in surprise when he saw her.

The colour rose in Sara's cheeks. As casually as she could manage she asked. 'Can I help?'

Marjorie looked as puzzled as Sara felt; she moved to Stephen's side. They were all waiting for Lucy, and she didn't disappoint.

Lucy cleared her throat. At that moment some instinct warned Stephen that Lucy was going to cause trouble, he lifted his hand in a half-hearted protest, but it was too late. Lucy's determined voice echoed across the room. 'Sara . . . Marjorie just mentioned you were in Stephen's office yesterday?'

Cautious, because no-one had yet explained what this was all about, she said. 'Yes, I went in there to put some papers on his desk.'

Lucy nodded. 'To cut things short, a small silver Georgian snuffbox is missing. Stephen uses it to store his stamps. He's certain it was on his desk yesterday, and now it's gone. We noticed it is missing because I asked Stephen to give me a stamp for his birthday card . . . ' She waved a white envelope in the air. ' . . . to save me going home for one. Did you happen to see it on the desk yesterday?'

Shock yielded to fury and the colour drained from Sara's face. 'Are you suggesting I stole it?' She seethed with anger and humiliation but tried to keep calm. Clenching her teeth, and with her nails digging into the palms of her hands, she'd never felt more angry in all her life.

Lucy hastened to pretend sympathy, but the ice-cold eyes gave her away.

'Of course not, but I'm sure you'll understand that we have to ask, however unpleasant it is for us.'

Sara snapped back. 'No, I don't understand. It sounds like you've made me your number one suspect!' Sara's natural reticence dissolved and her temper flared. Her whole body felt like an over-strung violin. She tried to keep some shreds of composure. Her voice was shaking with anger.

'It has nothing to do with me! I've been in Stephen's office a couple of times, and I've never even noticed a snuffbox.' Between thin lips she glared at Lucy, and her gaze swept Stephen and his mother angrily. 'I have never ever stolen anything in the whole of my life!!'

Sara's mouth was slightly open as she searched desperately for the right words; her eyes were huge and shadowy. She threw Stephen an angry look, and although there was shock in his face he remained silent. She also saw the frozen look of astonishment on Marjorie's face.

'Why would I put my reputation and that of my company at risk for the sake of a snuffbox? I have nothing to do with its loss. I suggest you make a more thorough search or look for an alternative solution.' Without waiting for a comment, she turned on her heels, and exited back out of the door.

She bent to put on her shoes; her hazel eyes were brimming with tears. A babble of loud voices issued from indoors. The door was flung open and Marjorie hurried towards her. She caught Sara's arm, as Sara was about to descend the steps. 'Sara! Please — I know you don't have anything to do with this. How dare Lucy even suggest such a thing!'

Sara brushed the tears away with the back of her hand, and although the breath was burning in her throat, she smiled at the older woman weakly. 'Thanks!'

'Stephen doesn't believe it either. Come back, Sara! Let's sort it out now.'

Sara shook her head. 'I'm sorry, but I can't. If I never see Lucy again, it will be too soon. I don't know why she dislikes me, but she does and it seems that Stephen is ready to believe her. Nothing can change the fact that she's just accused me of stealing.' She broke away and ran towards her car.

Loud, excited voices from the entrance hall drifted outside where Marjorie Dumont bleakly watched Sara's departing figure.

Sara sat in her car and waited until she stopped shaking. She tried to control her anger and wiped her eyes with the tissues from the glove compartment. She had to think straight; what was the correct thing to do? It wasn't just her problem; she was an employee. She took a deep breath and reached for her mobile phone. With a voice that was fighting to stay in control she explained to Brian what had just happened.

'What! I've never heard anything so idiotic in my life!' The roar in Brian's voice helped to bring a touch of normality back into her life. 'You're staying at the local pub, aren't you? Go there now. I'll join you there. It'll take me less than half an hour to be with you, I'm visiting a client not far away.' He muttered to himself, 'They must be completely mad!'

It was heartening to have his unwavering support. With a voice that was smothering a sob she said. 'I swear I didn't steal anything. I was alone in the office yesterday, but I don't even know what they're talking about. I don't remember ever seeing a snuff-box. I put the papers down on to the desk, and left.'

'You don't have to tell me that, Sara, I believe you.'

Sara did as Brian told her. She drove

back to the Smith's Arms, giving a fleeting thought to some gardening tools she'd left lying round, but someone else would have to collect them. Sitting on the edge of her bed, she covered her face with trembling hands and gave way to tears again. Her heart was like a lump of lead. Lucy had made Sara into a common thief in the eyes of Stephen and Marjorie and it left a very bitter taste in Sara's mouth. It was a memory that was hard to erase.

When Brian arrived, she explained once again what had happened. Sitting on the edge of her bed, hands between the legs of her jeans, with swollen eyes, her boss Brian, had never seen her look so desolate.

His round ruddy face was full of sympathy. 'How could they be so stupid? What kind of people are they? You'd cut off your hand before you took something that didn't belong to you. Know what, my girl? There is no reason you have to face them again. Pack your bags and get out of here! Go home! The work here is finished anyway. I'll get the foreman to tie up the loose ends.'

Biting her lips she looked at him. 'Can I? Just leave?'

He nodded. 'Why not?'

'It will look like I'm running away. What if they call the police and they want to question me?'

'For a snuffbox? Are you kidding? How much does something like that cost £80? £100? They know where they can find you. I'll tell them to phone me.'

'I'm sorry, Brian — I hope this doesn't damage the reputation of the company — but I didn't do it!'

'Sara, I believe you; how many times do I have to tell you? You've done nothing wrong! You've done a job, and an excellent one at that! You fulfilled the contract to the last dot. Stephen Dumont won't be stupid enough to say anything libellous about the company. I'll sort this out. What's he like? As a person?'

She stared down at her hands. She couldn't describe him other than she'd known him. 'He's young, professional, fair, and hard-working.'

'Then I see no problem. I'm going to talk to him. I'll make sure he realises the company is 100% behind you, and I'll tell him we decided that it's better for everyone concerned if you leave straight away, and our foreman clears up the last bits and pieces.'

A weight fell from her shoulders; Sara was relieved she wouldn't have to face them again or say goodbye. She felt a real ache about never seeing Stephen again; but how could she face them after today, it would always stand between them. It was better to leave like Brian suggested.

10

Brian sat facing Stephen. He was younger than Brian expected. 'Sara has completed all the work that needs her personal attention. It's better for her if she puts some space between this place and herself, after what's happened.'

Stephen's face was tense and the lines around his mouth were drawn. 'I understand that of course, but I'd like a chance to tell her personally that I have no doubt about her honesty.'

Brian replied quickly. 'Sara is one of the best employees I've ever had. She's reliable, hard-working, caring and honest; no-one could wish for a better colleague.'

Stephen nodded. 'Would . . . would you give me her address so that I can write a few words or at least phone her.'

Brian shifted in the chair. 'I can't give you her personal address without asking her for permission to do so, and anyway, I don't think it's a good idea at the moment, Mr Dumont. This business has knocked her for six; I've never seen her so upset. Give her some time to adjust, and then I'm sure it will be fine if you send her a few lines of support.'

'I'm going to suggest she goes on holiday; she usually takes a couple of weeks off at this time of the year. It will do her good to get away and relax. What about getting in touch with her in a month or so?'

Stephen's mouth looked even more pinched as he listened, but he was left no choice. He got up and held out his hand. 'I'm very sorry that the whole thing happened in the first place. I know the loss of the snuffbox had absolutely nothing to do with Miss Maxwell. She's done an excellent job and I'm 100% satisfied with the results. I can only recommend her . . . and your company, of course.'

Brian got up and took his hand. 'Has the snuffbox turned up?'

'No, but it wasn't important anyway. It certainly wasn't worth upsetting Sara like that. If it never turns up again, it won't bother me as much as the damage it's done.'

Brian got ready to leave. He paused; some instinct told him Stephen Dumont was a decent type of man. 'Why not send her a letter, via the office, in a couple of weeks.' The words didn't seem to achieve what Brian thought they would. The young man seemed just as despondent.

'Thank you for coming! I'll show you out.'

A couple of days later, Stephen stood for a moment after he'd closed the door on a visitor from the local authority. On his way back to the library, he hesitated and then knocked on Marjorie's sitting room door and went in.

She looked up at him and put the paper down. He had been so withdrawn during the last week and he looked drawn and worn-out. 'Hello, Stephen, like some tea?'

He shook his head and ran his hand down his face. 'I wanted to tell you that I'm going away tomorrow. I'm going to see if I can find Sara. Her boss thought it was better not to get in touch with her for a while, but I have to see her.'

Marjorie nodded understandingly. 'Good! I think you're right. I can't stop thinking about what happened. I've watched Lucy grow up, and she was almost like one of the family, but nothing can explain why she was so malicious and unkind to Sara. It was a cruel thing to do. We both know Sara would be incapable of doing something like that. I think jealousy drove Lucy to be so spiteful and unkind.' She paused. 'Has Lucy the right to be jealous? I don't want to interfere in your life, but I wondered.'

He shook his head. 'Lucy and I have gone around together, or in a crowd ever since I can remember. I admit that at one time I did think about settling down with Lucy permanently, because she was there, I knew her and I thought it would be enough, but I never talked to her about it, and officially we were never more than good friends. Then Sara came on to the scene and changed everything. I presume Lucy sensed her position was endangered. I think the snuffbox was just a last desperate attempt by her to blacken Sara in my eyes.'

Marjorie touched his arm briefly. 'I'm sorry! Sorry for the way things have worked out for you and Sara and I'm sorry for Lucy too. She seems to have been determined to marry you. How is she, do you know?'

He shrugged. 'I've been in touch with her father once or twice. He's a bit stiff with me; probably thinks it is my entire fault, which it is in a way. He says the doctor thinks she's on the brink of a nervous breakdown. He recommended a change of scenery for a while and her dad is already busy organising a long winter cruise in the Caribbean!' He gave his mother a wry smile. 'Sometimes I think Lucy would have been a nicer person if everyone hadn't fallen over themselves to remove every stone in her path. She's never had to fight for anything — that means she can't cope if her wishes aren't fulfilled; like a spoiled child.'

His mother asked what she'd been longing to know for a while. 'So I presume that you are in love with Sara?'

He nodded. 'Yes.'

'Good! I like her very much. It is important that you marry the right person Stephen, if you end up with the wrong partner it would be hell. Sara is right for you. She's a lovely girl; she's hardworking, intelligent and caring. You have to find her and clear up all these misunderstandings.'

'I want to; I wanted to from the moment she left, but her boss told me it was better to wait, and write her a letter in a couple of weeks. I don't know where she lives, I had no alternative but to wait, but I'm fed up with waiting. I have to see her. I'm going to see her boss again and I'll persuade him to tell me where she is, or if he doesn't perhaps I can persuade the foreman to help.'

She smiled, 'Oh, Stephen! Sara needed reassurance straight away, not a couple of weeks later. Her boss doesn't know what he's talking about. Every day counts! Men don't understand women at all. You can do better than that!'

His tight expression relaxed into a weak smile. 'Once I have her address I'll do my damned best to persuade her I need her with me for the rest of my life!'

With an answering smile of amusement, she said, 'Let's think! I'm trying to recall things she told me . . . she mentioned her father was called Arthur and I also know she was born in Flax Bourton. It won't be difficult for you to find the address of Arthur Maxwell in Flax Bourton via your computer, will it? Her parents know where she is and you'll have to persuade them to give you her address. If you tell them you have to see her urgently for personal reasons, they'll help.'

'You're right!' He grabbed her and gave her a quick kiss. 'Thanks, Mum! Why didn't I talk to you earlier? Yours are the only sensible words I've heard since she left! I was beginning to think I'd go mad if I had to wait much longer!'

11

The whole of last week had been miserable. Brian had kept her busy with office work, but it didn't succeed in banishing her longings. The men had finished their work at Knowles House and cleared it of their tools and machines. There were no more connections — Knowles House was now just an ex-customer. Brian had persuaded her to take some leave and she decided it was a good idea. She still spent too much time checking things that had to do with Knowles House. Her longings for Stephen would all fade in time; they had to.

Sara had spent the morning shopping; but she ended up with nothing new, and could scarcely remember what she'd seen. It was merely a good way of passing the time, being among crowds of people helped to divert her thoughts.

She'd seen a special offer for 10 days in Hong Kong in the newspaper and had intended to go to the travel agent and get details, but she'd even forgotten to do that, and now she was home again, empty handed.

She didn't notice Stephen. He'd parked his car under some trees on the opposite side of the road in the quiet cul-de-sac where she lived. Her small flat was on the ground floor and she'd been happy there ever since she moved in. She liked the district and she knew her neighbours quite well. The elderly lady next door always took in her parcels, and kept an eye on things when she wasn't home.

Stephen had been waiting a couple of hours already. He'd knocked at her door without success, and then went back to his BMW to sit and wait for her return. Her mother told him Sara was talking about going on a short holiday, but hadn't fixed anything yet.

When she arrived home mid-afternoon, Stephen could observe her without being noticed himself. She was dressed formally in a modern suit. It skimmed her slender figure and a rust-coloured top peeped out at the collar of the jacket. Her hair glowed a rich auburn in the afternoon sunlight. She looked delicate and ethereal.

He was enchanted by her looks and the way she carried herself. No-one would ever guess this attractive young woman did a job that was physically demanding. He noticed she looked tired and disconsolate.

She walked up the short pathway to her door and fumbled in her capacious leather bag for the key. Her high heels echoed on the short pathway.

He got out of his car and pocketed his own keys before he walked determinedly in her direction. By the time she'd turned the key in the lock, he was within distance. He called her name and she twisted around. His voice caught her completely off guard, and she stared at him tongue-tied and disbelieving.

'Sara, can I talk to you a minute?' He wasn't certain of what his reception would be like; his voice was uptight.

Her hazel eyes widened as she tried to adjust to his presence. 'Stephen?' The colour had drained from her face; she was as white as a sheet. 'What are you doing here? How do you know where I live?'

'A long story, but basically I got your address from your mother.'

'My mother? You've met my mother?'

'Yes, I drove to your parents' address this morning. Your dad wasn't there, he was out at work, but your mother and I had a long chat, and I think I convinced her that I needed to talk to you badly. She seemed to know who I was, because she recognised my name straight away.'

Sara nodded. 'I usually tell them about where I'm working and about what I'm doing. They've always been interested.'

'Your mother sized me up, and then she told me where you were. I like her, by the way — she seems to be a very nice person. You have her eyes.'

The colour came flooding back. 'Do I?' The conversation seemed unreal, she grappled with some remaining shreds of normality as she stared at his face.

He nodded. 'When I got there, she'd just taken some scones out of the oven.' He smiled, and her heart turned over. 'I think I must have eaten at least four of them while we were talking!'

Confusion was still dominant, and she was too startled to do more than look at him mutely.

He held out his hands in a gesture of apology and plunged in. 'Sara, I'm sorry about what happened! I know you had nothing to do with the disappearance of the snuffbox. I never believed it, not for a single second. I could kill Lucy for putting you on the spot like she did. I didn't know what she was going to do — otherwise I would have stopped her. By the time I'd recovered from the surprise of it all it was too late. You had left.'

She looked down at the key as she pulled it out of the lock; it gave her a chance to drag her glance away from his face for a few seconds. She swallowed a lump in her throat and pushed open the door. 'You'd better come inside.'

She led the way through the tiny square-shaped hall into a small sitting room; Stephen followed. He seemed to fill the small room with his presence. She put her handbag down on the floor, next to the sideboard, and crossed the room to open the French windows.

A small patio was dotted with glazed pots full of green plants and an open book lay face down on a garden chair.

She was glad the room looked attractive. It was an irrelevant thought, because he'd never come again — once he'd got through his apologies she'd never see him again. She gestured to one of the chairs. 'Sit down, please! Would you like something to drink — coffee, tea, or something stronger?'

He shook his head impatiently. 'You forgive me?'

She lifted her chin and met his gaze. 'What for? You weren't the one who said I'd stolen the snuffbox!' Her lashes brushed her cheeks and she looked down, unable to stare at him for too long; she moistened her dried lips and looked up again. 'Brian told me that you didn't think I was a thief. You didn't have to make the extra journey to make an apology. There is nothing to forgive; no need for an apology.'

They were facing each other, and close enough that when he reached forward to take her hand Sara was so busy watching his face she had no chance to think about if she should tear it away or not. She was totally confused by the effect the touch of his hand had on her; she gave in and left her hand where it was. She couldn't tear her glance from him either, his nearness was overwhelming. She could hear her heartbeat hammering away in her ears, and she heard his quick intake of breath.

As he fondled her hand, shivers of

wanting flooded through her; she did her best not to show any reaction. She tried to concentrate on what he was saying.

'I was so astonished by Lucy's behaviour and wondering how I could save the situation that I didn't register you were leaving till it was too late. Then Lucy started shouting and making a scene about how you'd changed the people at Knowles House, telling me how I was neglecting her, and how she'd wasted her whole life waiting for me.

'At first I just tried to calm her, but she got more hysterical when I said I was sure you had nothing to do with the disappearance of the snuffbox. Her fury knew no bounds, and I soon figured it was some kind of personal vendetta against you. I decided the best thing was to get her home to her father as soon as possible — he's the only one who can handle her when she's in a frenzy.

'I couldn't let her drive herself; she'd have driven headlong into a tree or done something equally as stupid. A state of nervous hysterics is a mild description of what she was like! My mother told me how she couldn't stop you either.

'By the time I'd driven Lucy home, explained to her father what had happened, and driven back to the Smith's Arms, you'd already packed and left, and when I got back to Knowles House your boss was already waiting to see me. He was clearly mad as a bull about what happened, and advised me to leave you alone for a bit.' Stephen was silent for a moment. 'I've found that's impossible, because I can't live without you.'

She was taken aback for a moment, but then felt happiness begin to bubble inside. She was coming alive for the first time since leaving Knowles House.

'I had to tell you what I've been longing to say for weeks. I love you! I'm not sure if you want to hear it after what's happened. I intended to ask you how you felt about me before the work at the house finished but I left it too late and everything blew up around us.' His hand slid up to her shoulder and with the help of the other he gathered her into his arms until they were inches apart. 'Do I have a chance Sara? Do you care about me a little?'

Her communication skills seemed to have disappeared as she stared up into his face. She could only nod, and she buried herself against his chest. He lifted her chin with one finger and she felt the heady sensation of his lips.

This time the kiss wasn't a gentle one; it was hungry and urgent. She wasn't surprised when her own response was just as eager and demanding. She saw delight in his eyes, and then he reclaimed her lips, he crushed her to him again. Her whole being was flooded with happiness and desire for him.

He had a sensuous look on his face and then he gave her an irresistibly devastating smile. 'Wow! I've been living with uncertainty for too long. But you love me, I can tell.'

Her smile was smug with delight. 'I have for a while now, but I was never sure if you were Lucy's or not! I tried to ignore you, but it got more difficult as the time went on. In the end, I was glad to escape without having to say goodbye. I never expected to see you again, even though I couldn't stand the thought of you and Lucy together.'

'I've never loved Lucy. She was a friend. Lucy has been around as long as I remember, and I admit I might have drifted into an arrangement if you hadn't come into my life. I fell in love with you and knew I needed you to make my life complete and make me happy, really happy.'

She stroked his cheek with the back of her hand, delighting in the feeling of being able to touch him; he turned his head and kissed her fingers. 'It would have been very stupid to marry anyone if you didn't love them. I didn't think you were a stupid man.'

'You started to worm your way into my heart from the first day you came into my library with your plans. You took possession of it without me noticing, and I suddenly realised I couldn't imagine my life without you any more. I think that after a while if you had come to me with a suggestion to put a cage of monkeys in the middle of the lawn, I would have done it!'

She laughed, freed of all the anger and all the pain of the last couple of weeks. 'I wish I'd known that at the time, I would have expanded my ideas!'

'You have the rest of your life to bombard me with plans.'

She beamed. 'Really? That's wonderful.'

'I wasn't sure how you felt about Alan, but I was determined to tell you how I felt before you left — then Lucy's performance messed everything up.'

Sara's eyes glowed and the tired expression had disappeared. Stephen rejoiced silently, because he knew that it was because of how she felt about him.

'Have you found it — the snuffbox?'

He picked her up and swung her

around. 'Who cares about a damned snuffbox? I have a feeling we never will.' He fell back into the nearby chair and it tilted perilously, before righting itself. He positioned her across his lap. 'To be honest, I think Lucy had something to do with its disappearance, but I don't intend to waste time on thinking about it. I want to make more important plans! Firstly are you really prepared to take me on, and Knowles House — I'm afraid we go together! Will you marry me?'

The breath caught in her throat but she cupped his face between her hands and kissed him. Without hesitation she said, 'Yes!'

His eyes met hers and the pact was settled.

He looked happier than she'd ever seen. 'Wonderful! That's settled. Next, how do you feel about your present job? As long as you are within travelling distance of Knowles I'd encourage you to carry on doing your job because I know you enjoy your work, but if you spent more time away from me than at home, I'll find it hard to bear.'

She laughed softly. 'You don't even know what it's like to live with me yet, once you do, you may be glad to get rid of me from time to time!'

His answering kiss gave his answer. 'Impossible! What I'm trying to say is would you mind very much if you only took on jobs within the immediate vicinity? Or perhaps you could establish your own company; that would be even better! But I don't want to be the one who stopped you doing what you want to.'

She shook her head and tightened her grip around his shoulder. 'I'll stick with Brian for as long as it's sensible. I'm sure he'll let me handle the work within a fair travelling distance of Knowles House if that's what I want, or I'll see if there is a local firm who'll take me on. When we have children, I'll be quite prepared to concentrate on them and Knowles House for a while. If I can't work as a garden designer, I can take some of the work involved with running the events off your shoulders.'

He looked dumbfounded. 'Children?'

She chuckled. 'Of course. We need a half-dozen to ensure the future of Knowles House.'

He threw back his head and chuckled. 'Sara that is a wonderful idea. Two perhaps, or three, but six . . . ? And I want you to myself for a while first. By the way, I guarantee that my mother will be over the moon when she hears. She's been your biggest fan right from the beginning.'

He kissed her forehead. 'And I understand why!' He paused for a moment. 'Knowles House is waiting for you — you've already begun to reshape the garden. Wouldn't it be a great idea for us to be the first couple to get married there, before it's officially opened to the general public?'

Sara was startled. 'Heavens!'

'Christmas or springtime?'

'Give me time to think about it! I have to consider whether Knowles House would be too overwhelming for my parents.'

186

He looked philosophical. 'I think you underestimate your mother. I think the only thing that matters to her is that you find happiness. I don't think any of the trappings count at all. If your father is as nice as your mother, I don't see any problems. They want what you want. We wouldn't need to invite half the county, only the people who are important to you and the ones who are important to me.'

'Don't worry about filling the ball-room with people who are not really important. It's up to us how we organise the day. I only thought Knowles House would be good because it's my home, your future home, and also your former workplace, but if you want to marry in the local registry office, that's fine by me.'

Sara's happiness showed in her face and was mirrored in her eyes. Everything had changed, but it had all changed for the better — and this was just the beginning.

We do hope that you have enjoyed reading this large print book.

Did you know that all of our titles are available for purchase?

We publish a wide range of high quality large print books including:
Romances, Mysteries, Classics
General Fiction
Non Fiction and Westerns

Special interest titles available in large print are:
The Little Oxford Dictionary
Music Book, Song Book
Hymn Book, Service Book

Also available from us courtesy of Oxford University Press:
Young Readers' Dictionary
(large print edition)
Young Readers' Thesaurus
(large print edition)

For further information or a free brochure, please contact us at:
Ulverscroft Large Print Books Ltd.,
The Green, Bradgate Road, Anstey,
Leicester, LE7 7FU, England.
Tel: (00 44) **0116 236 4325**
Fax: (00 44) **0116 234 0205**

A MIDSUMMER DREAM

Janet Thomas

Victoria Williams is photographing wildlife on the Cornish cliffs when she meets Bron Macdonald and becomes drawn into his world of film-making. During the shooting of an old Cornish legend, Vicky's integrity is threatened by a woman's jealousy. Seemingly insuperable obstacles arise between her and Bron, but are resolved. However, despite their reconciliation, Vicky must choose between loyalty to her sister and her love for Bron. How will she resolve her dilemma? Must she let Bron go?

COLLISION COURSE WITH LOVE

Sarah Evans

Widowed for over a year, Gabby Balfour decides it's time she moved on. She emigrates to Australia intent on new beginnings, but feels guilty that she's alive while her husband's not. When she meets gorgeous entrepreneur Sam Donovan the attraction is instant, yet she's scared to fall in love again, of being vulnerable and open to the pain of loss. But Sam helps her find closure on her grief and guilt, and the courage to embrace a new love.

LUCREZIA'S SECRET

Toni Anders

In England, Lacey's uncle, a perfumier, wants to re-create Lucrezia Borgia's own perfume. He sends his niece to Capri to obtain the secret formula. Aware of the danger that her mission might be foiled, Lacey fears that there's nobody she can trust — especially when there's a scruffy young man who seems to be stalking her. But when Scott, the helpful Texan, befriends Lacey, will she find that her suspicions about the unkempt and scarily ubiquitous Rob are all wrong?

RACHEL'S COMING HOME

Gillian Villiers

When her parents run into difficulties running their boarding kennels, Rachel Collington decides to resign from her job and return home to help out. The first customer she encounters is arrogant Philip Milligan, who is nowhere near as friendly as his two collies. Gradually though, he begins to thaw — but just as Rachel is wondering if she has misjudged him, it seems that someone is intent on sabotaging the Kennels' reputation.

HEALING LOVE

Cara Cooper

Dr James Frayne's personal life is in meltdown and it is beginning to affect his work. Becky, his Practice Manager, is deeply concerned and wants to help. But Dr James cannot afford to let her in on his secret — if she discovers what's troubling him, it could lose him his job. When his cold efficiency and her powers of deduction collide, sparks fly and emotions are stirred — changing both their lives forever . . .